T0167306

Flowers of the Forest

A novel by

JAMES HENRY GRAHAM

The Flow'rs o' the Forest that fought aye the
foremost,
The prime o' our land lie cauld i' the clay.
---Old Scottish Lament.

iUniverse, Inc.
Bloomington

Flowers of the Forest

Copyright © 2011 by James Henry Graham

All rights reserved. No part of this book may be used or reproduced by any means, graphic, electronic, or mechanical, including photocopying, recording, taping or by any information storage retrieval system without the written permission of the publisher except in the case of brief quotations embodied in critical articles and reviews.

This is a work of fiction. All of the characters, names, incidents, organizations, and dialogue in this novel are either the products of the author's imagination or are used fictitiously.

iUniverse books may be ordered through booksellers or by contacting:

iUniverse
1663 Liberty Drive
Bloomington, IN 47403
www.iuniverse.com
1-800-Authors (1-800-288-4677)

Because of the dynamic nature of the Internet, any web addresses or links contained in this book may have changed since publication and may no longer be valid. The views expressed in this work are solely those of the author and do not necessarily reflect the views of the publisher, and the publisher hereby disclaims any responsibility for them.

Any people depicted in stock imagery provided by Thinkstock are models, and such images are being used for illustrative purposes only.

Certain stock imagery © Thinkstock.

ISBN: 978-1-4620-2527-5 (sc)
ISBN: 978-1-4620-2528-2 (e)

Printed in the United States of America

iUniverse rev. date: 9/13/2011

Prologue

THE IMPACT OF GALE FORCE WINDS caused Norman Burke's '38 Nash to fishtail on the icy street. Steering into the skid, Norman nosed the sedan into a snowdrift.

"I'll get out and give it a push," the soldier in the passenger seat said, reaching for a door handle.

"Nah," Norman said, "Sit tight. I'll rock 'er out."

Norman began changing gears -- from reverse to forward and back again -- causing the car to rock back and forth until the chains on the rear wheels allowed the big automobile to free itself.

"Hey! Good driving pal. I thought we were in the rhubarb for sure." The soldier patted him on the shoulder before tucking his chin into the collar of his greatcoat and resuming a nap that began shortly after he entered the car.

Norman worked as a baggage handler at the Canadian National Railways passenger terminal in Edmonton. After he had finished his shift he had gone into the depot for a cup of coffee and was batting the breeze with some red caps when a soldier's predicament was brought to his attention. The man was on leave and trying to reach a house on the City Limit Road, but none of the taxi drivers in attendance would chance a trip over a route notorious for large, road-crossing snowdrifts. Norman lived in Calder, a community whose northern boundary was defined by the City Limit Road and he felt equal to the task as his car was equipped with chains on its driving wheels and two 50 lb. bags of cement in the trunk for ballast.

The depot was full of soldiers that evening so a redcap guided Norman to a uniformed man sleeping on a bench. When Norman shook him awake, the soldier tensed and his eyes flew open. He stared around the room or several moments before looking up at Norman, who introduced himself and offered to drive him to his destination. The soldier was gratified by the offer and rose to his feet, lifted the strap of his kit bag over his shoulder, and followed his benefactor out of the building.

Now, tense from keeping his car on the road, Norman envied his passenger in his winter issue clothing with the earflaps of his khaki headgear tied down over his ears. It occurred to him that his passenger's headgear was similar to that worn by Home Service troops – a.k.a. Zombies -- who had been conscripted into the armed services, but had exercised an option not to serve in a combat zone. Norman, who had washed out of basic training after losing three fingers on his right hand to a malfunctioning grenade, thought: 'Dammit,' am I knockin' myself out fer a goddamned Zombie? Maybe I should dump him right here and go home.'

After freeing the car they proceeded north for several miles with windblown snow glowing in the headlights and overwhelming the wipers. Norman reduced his speed until he turned west on to the City Limit Road, an avenue in the lee of a shelter break that extended for several miles. With enhanced visibility, he felt confident enough to increase his speed.

"Make a right at that road." The soldier sat forward and pointed a gloved finger at an approaching sign.

Norman braked cautiously and slowed for the turn. The car slid until its wheels gained purchase on a snow-covered lane that led away from the main road. The byway took them through a stand of denuded poplars, whose skeletal branches tapped out Morse code-like rhythms on the vehicle's roof as it made its way toward a sheltered clearing containing a two-storey house and several outbuildings.

"This is it." The soldier said, a note of excitement in his voice.

Norman brought the sedan to a stop under a yard light at the foot of a shoveled path. He shifted the gear lever to neutral and grinned at the soldier. "Well. We made it."

"All thanks to you pal" the soldier smiled and opened the lapels of his greatcoat. Norman's eyes widened at the array of campaign ribbons revealed above the soldier's left breast pocket as the man retrieved a leather wallet.

"Nah. Keep yer money."

"No, no," the soldier insisted, waving a wad of bills. "Take it. Christ...you earned it. Driving me out here. Night like this."

"I seen all that fruit salad on yer chest. Where'd ya serve?"

"Italy...most the time. I don't usually wear all this stuff but I've been on a war bond tour."

"My kid brother's over there," Norman said. "Least I can do is give you a lift home. Besides, I owe you an apology. Because a' yer hat,' I took you fer a Zombie."

The soldier laughed. "Somebody lifted my lid on the train and I ended up with this number. But...don't get me wrong. I'm starting to think that the Zombies have the right idea. I can't count the number of times I've kicked my own ass for volunteering for that shit storm over there."

He tugged a sheaf of bills from his wallet and peeled off two tens, which he held up to Norman.

"Take the money. You earned it. Buy your wife some perfume or something. I didn't get any shut-eye on the train because the bloody dice just kept rolling' my way. I got on in the 'Peg with five bucks and now I got more cabbage than Carter's got pills."

Norman sat still and didn't speak as the soldier reached over and tucked the bills into a side pocket of his leather windbreaker.

"I'll wait until someone comes to the door... wouldn't want to leave you stranded out here."

"Good man." The soldier stepped out of the car and opened the rear passenger door. Reaching into the back seat, he retrieved his kit bag and slammed the door shut. He slung the bag over his shoulder and made his way between the waist-high piles of snow that bordered the walk. When the front door opened he turned and gave the driver a thumbs-up.

Norman gave the horn a short beep and engaged the clutch. The vehicle moved forward inscribing a u-turn in the snow as it made its way back toward the main road.

She met him at the door, pulled him into the house and wrapped her arms around him. "Oh my God. You're safe. Come in. Come in. I just fixed some supper." She held him at arm's length and looked at him with tears in her eyes. "I can't believe you're really here."

"You here alone?" He looked around as she helped him shed his greatcoat in the entranceway.

"I'm the only one here now. Sit down," she said and pointed to a chair in the kitchen. "I'll get you a plate and some cutlery." He smiled, as he watched her busy herself in the familiar kitchen.

After dinner, they sat and talked for hours. When his eyes began involuntarily closing, and his chin kept dropping to his chest, she led him to his old bedroom.

"Sleep as late as you like," she said and left him.

Sometime in the early morning hours, he felt her warm body slip into his bed. As he pulled her to him, she moaned hungrily and began showering his face with kisses.

Sometime later she whispered to him, "Wake up soldier, you have a train to catch."

"Just few more minutes," he murmured and reached for her.

"Sorry Honey, but you've got to get up now. Wake up!"

He awoke. Neither in the arms of a lover nor in the comfort of a warm bed, but rather in a chilling landscape that caused him to close his eyes tightly in an attempt to recapture the dream. When he opened them again, he groaned at the sight of his snow-covered surroundings.

A pint milk bottle lay within inches of his right hand; its contents visible through the clear glass. He made an effort to retrieve it but his hand would not move. He concentrated on capturing the container, but his hand remained unresponsive. It became apparent to him that he couldn't feel or control any of his extremities.

He lay with his head propped against the carcass of a discarded sofa, which he had dragged it into a large packing case to provide shelter from the falling snow, and looked to the remains of the fire that had been so robust when he had fallen asleep beside it. He watched it flicker weakly amid piles of combustible material.

Several days earlier, when the temperature had dropped into minus double digits, Stoney --

a name given him by some Calder pool hall lay bouts -- had sought shelter where he could find it. A sympathetic machinist had let him bed down in an unused tool crib in a secluded area of the roundhouse for several nights and he had spent the previous night in a caboose at the east end of the CN rail yard. He had wandered around the extension tracks and sidings until he spotted a way-freight crew switching a caboose and several boxcars into a siding. After the crew departed with the locomotive and water car, he clambered up the steps of the caboose.

Happy at finding the door unlocked, he entered and stood for several moments luxuriating in the warm air. He opened the double-latched door of the cast-iron stove, reached into an adjacent bin and picked up a number of briquettes, which he fed onto the glowing embers. A drawer, on the built-in desk, yielded a paper switch list, which he curled into a cone and, removing the glass chimney of the wall-mounted lamp, transferred a flame from the stove to its wick.

Lamplight revealed his face and the network of broken blood vessels that traversed his cheeks and the bridge of his nose. Quarter-sized patches of peeling skin, encrusted blood and a spotty growth of gray whiskers covered his cheeks and chin. His eyes were rheumy and red-rimmed.

Stoney replaced the chimney on the lamp, pulled up a small wooden armchair, and sat down at the desk. He tugged his woolen mitts off with his teeth and withdrew a pint bottle of milk from a side pocket of his army surplus greatcoat. He placed it on the desktop before removing a flat brown bottle from another pocket. He poured off some of the milk and added rubbing alcohol from the brown bottle. Fixing the round cardboard cap into the top of the milk bottle, he secured it with a thumb and shook the components into a concoction popularly known as 'steam.' Removing the cap, he smelled the concoction, swirled it around, and raised it to his lips. He sat for some time, sipping from the bottle, before setting it on the table.

The effects of the steam, and the growing warmth of the caboose, lulled him to a state of drowsiness and he loosened his clothing and arranged himself on the floor near the stove. He drifted into a fitful sleep, frequently interrupted by a series of snorts and gasps and, at times, a temporary cessation of breathing.

When the wall clock indicated seven a.m., the door opened to admit a man in bulky winter garb holding a switch lantern. His eyes roamed the caboose's interior as he elevated his chin and wrinkled his nose. Unaware of Stoney, who lay in the shadow of the desk, he lifted the bottle of steam and sniffed it.

"Jee-suz Kee-rist! Goddamn rubbies!"

Stoney stirred, raised his head and stared uncomprehendingly at the man for several moments. Then his eyes fixed on the milk bottle in the man's hand and he swayed to his feet and rose to his full height. The shorter man uttered a surprised yelp and backed away from the apparition that loomed up before him.

"That's mine. Give it to me!" Stoney rasped and wrested the bottle from the switchman. He pushed the terrified man back against the wall where he slid to a sitting position on the floor. The man held his breath as he watched Stoney move to the table, carefully close the bottle and lower it into a side-pocket of his greatcoat. He picked up the army-issue web belt, which he had placed on the desk, wrapped it around his waist and fastened the interlocking brass buckle to hold the button less garment closed. He pulled up his collar, wrapped a long woolen scarf around it, tugged his toque down over his ears and pulled on his mitts. Stoney's garments were shiny with dirt but they provided him with a modicum of protection from the cold. Under his long greatcoat he wore several layers of clothing; long underwear, two shirts, two sweaters and a pair of threadbare suit pants under army issue wool serge trousers. His rag-wrapped feet were stuffed into a pair of broken-down sheepskin-lined flying boots that were secured around his ankles with binder twine.

Without a glance at the switchman, he made his way out of the caboose and stepped down the metal steps to the rail bed as a drag of slow moving rail cars were moving on the next track. Quickening his pace, he reached out and grasped the iron ladder of a passing boxcar and pulled himself up until his feet cleared the ground. Clinging to the ladder he flailed his feet until his boots found purchase on the iron rungs.

The drag slowly made its way to the western end of the yard where it was switched on to the main line. As it left the confines of the yard it began to pick up speed and Stoney prepared himself for a dismount. His layered clothing and a snow bank prevented serious injury from his heavy landing and, after he rolled to a stop, he checked the bottle in his pocket and was relieved to find that the cap had remained in place.

When the running lights of the caboose disappeared into the ice fog and the rhythmic clacking of steel wheels faded, he regained his feet and scaled the embankment. He crossed the tracks to the switch tender's shanty -- which he knew would be vacant for several hours until the day crew started sending westbound trains from the yard -- but the door was locked with a CNR padlock. Not having the switch key that would unlock it, Stoney circled the structure for another means of access. Finding none, he turned away and made his way into blowing snow in the direction of the Calder dump, a place where he could assemble a shelter from an abundance of construction cast-offs, and start a fire from the flammable detritus that littered the site.

Now, in the cold grey morning, he lay in the nuisance ground. His eyes rolled skyward and a barely audible croak escaped his lips.

"So that's it then. That's all you've got for me."

Part One

Chapter 1 – Billy Jurva

Soviet Karelia, Summer 1923

VAIKO JURVA WAS BUILDING TO THE climax of his speech when the Russian shot him. Vaiko stared down at the blossoming red stain on his white shirt, fell to his knees, and collapsed on the deck of the hayrack that had functioned as his platform. A handful of papers escaped his hand and, picked up by a breeze, were scattered across the farmyard.

The Russian, a low-level constable who had been detailed to keep an eye on the North Americans, stared at the pistol in his hand as if it had acted on its own. His jaw dropped and his round face began to perspire as members of Vaiko's audience turned and began to move toward him. He dropped the pistol as if it were red hot. "Nyet, nyet." He shook his head vigorously and waved his hands signifying that he hadn't meant to discharge the firearm.

The constable, who had been honoured at being assigned to supervise this group of émigrés, had boasted of how he would cow the newcomers with the iron discipline of the Soviet Union and, of course, his own importance. For their part, the North Americans were not at all impressed by the apparatchik. They ignored his attempts to impose his authority on them and, even worse, they treated him with a casual contempt that both puzzled and infuriated him.

When they had gathered to hear the troublemaker Jurva speak that day, the constable had decided to make his move. He had intended to fire the pistol over Jurva's head to silence him, and then bring the assemblage under his control but his plan went awry when the ancient revolver discharged as he was lifting it, sending a bullet directly to Vaiko's chest.

"Get that sorry sumbitch." Arnie Kallio, a farmer from North Dakota, said as he led a number of men toward the Russian.

"Lookit him," Matti Kempainnen, a lumberjack from the Ottawa Valley, said, "he's pissing in his pants."

Another man walked up to the group and said: "Vaiko's dead. Let's string this son-of-a-bitch up." A roar of approval greeted the suggestion and the crowd carried the functionary up onto the back of a grain wagon and pulled it under a large oak. They were fixing a noose around the man's neck when a long-nosed sedan entered the farmyard. Two uniformed men sprang out and made for the wagon. A man in civilian clothes emerged from the rear passenger compartment and followed at a more leisurely pace.

The uniformed men elbowed their way through the assemblage and one raised a gloved hand, gesturing for the North Americans to release the constable. Reluctantly, Matti removed the noose from the reprieved man's head and propelled him toward the back of the wagon with a kick. One of the uniformed men caught him before he hit the ground.

The Russian civilian wore a leather trench coat over a tweed suit and peered from under the brim of a wide-brimmed fedora. As he approached the group at the wagon, he held up one of the papers that had flown from Vaiko's hand.

"A petition," he declared in fluent English. "What a tragedy. A man of immense talents…a natural leader…is slain while attempting to improve conditions for his fellow man. Let me assure you, that this fellow," he indicated the constable, "will be punished to the full extent of the law. I realize that you Wild West fellows favour summary justice, but the Soviet Union believes in due process."

"What about the demands on that petition?" A farmer from Saskatchewan spoke up. "We came here because we were told we could farm and set up lumber mills without interference from the government. All we've gotten so far is a load of bureaucratic bullshit."

"Gentlemen, gentlemen. I, Vladimir Kosmynko, Commissar for the Northern District, assure you that I have been assigned to this department to facilitate the agreements made by the Soviet Union to you...and vice versa."

While the main group was clustered around the grain wagon, a number of women attended to Vaiko. Lylli Koivisto looked up to see Vaiko's twenty-two year old son, Toivo, emerging from the barn wielding a sickle. He was making for the crowd at the wagon when she intercepted him.

"Toivo, what are you doing?"

"I'm gonna get that Russian bastard who shot my dad." He wiped away a tear with the back of a hand.

"It's too late for that." Lylli said. "The police have him."

"The police? He's with the police. Don't you see? It's a setup. They've been after Vaiko for months. They didn't like him riling up the immigrants."

"Toivo," Lylli gripped his arms. "You are in danger now. You must leave the country. The Bolsheviks have a bad habit of going after family members of dissidents and it is well known that you have been Vaiko's good right hand through all of this. Tonight, Arnie and Tauno will take you to the Finnish border. I will write to your family when I know that you are safe."

That evening Toivo Jurva left the Karelian collective farm and began a lifetime of planning revenge on anything Russian.

The Karelian adventure had come to Vaiko's attention in 1922. He had come upon an article in the Saskatoon Star-Phoenix detailing a Soviet plan to settle North American farmers and lumber workers, of Finnish descent, in Karelia, a Soviet territory located between Russia and Finland. The deal offered free land and the promise of an idyllic socialistic lifestyle in the forests and farms of the region.

Vaiko had immigrated to Canada in the spring of 1911 with his new bride Kaarina, his ten-year-old son Toivo (from a previous marriage) and his sixteen-year-old brother-in-law, Mikko Perala. The family came to claim up on 160 acres of free land in the Coteau Hills of southern Saskatchewan. Their homestead was located in an area appropriately called Rock Point.

From the proceeds of the sale of his dairy farm, near Gackle North Dakota, Vaiko purchased a smallholding with a cottage, barn, and several outbuildings, near the town of Dunblane. He considered Kaarina too frail for life on an undeveloped homestead and, against her wishes, relegated her to the cottage until suitable accommodations were available on the homestead.

With the help of Toivo and Mikko -- popularly known as 'Mingo' -- Vaiko broke soil, seeded a wheat crop, and erected a sod house and several outbuildings on the homestead. Grasshoppers ravaged the first year's crop. A subsequent crop, while damaged by hail, was partially salvageable. Vaiko made money in 1913 and broke even in 1914. In 1915 he brought in a bumper crop.

In 1916, at twenty-one years of age, Mingo felt

the urge to move on and try something other than farming. Toivo was by then a sturdy and capable fourteen-year old and Vaiko was financially able to hire extra help for the harvest so Mingo cashed out and caught a train to Alberta.

Over the ensuing years, dust storms, grasshoppers, hail, early frost, and a crippling drought in 1917, caused Vaiko to admit defeat and retreat to the Dunblane acreage. He gave up his homestead and sold his livestock except for one Jersey milk cow. Kaarina added the Jersey's output to that of her flock of chickens, and established a business selling butter, milk, cream and eggs to the residents of Dunblane and area. Kaarina, whose health had improved in the Coteau Hills, became the family breadwinner. A slight woman with an ethereal beauty and not nearly as fragile as she looked, Kaarina charmed her customers into buying her farm-fresh produce.

When a local teacher married and left her post, Kaarina applied to fill the vacancy. The local board accepted her North Dakota teaching certificate, and soon she was bringing more money into the household. In 1919, she paused to give birth to a son who was christened Wilho, but henceforth known as 'Billy.'

Vaiko worked as a non-paid organizer for a farmer's union but it was an occupation that brought in no revenue and the fact that his wife supported him made him feel diminished in the eyes of the community. Although he enjoyed spending time with his small son, he knew he had to do something to regain a sense of worth. He pursued the Soviet offering.

Soviet Russia had backed the Red Finns in the Finnish Civil War of 1918 and Vaiko held the Bolsheviks in high regard. Through contacts with Red Finns in Winnipeg, he made arrangements to accept the Karelian offer. Toivo, who had left home to work on a horse ranch, joined his father and they departed Canada in 1922. Their plan was to establish a farm and then send for Kaarina and Billy.

Several weeks after the departure of her husband and stepson, Kaarina was collecting eggs in the old barn when a rusty nail punctured her foot. After early treatment failed to stop the resulting infection, she wrote to Vaiko, asking that he and Toivo return home. Her letter crossed in the mail with one from him in which he extolled the virtues of Karelia and assured her that he would send for her and their son as soon as he received an allocation of land. It was to be his first and last communication.

When local care didn't improve her condition, Kaarina was admitted to a hospital in Saskatoon. Her older sister Anya, who had travelled from North Dakota to minister to her sister, brought her a letter from Lylli Koivisto, which informed them of Vaiko's fate and of Toivo's decision to remain in Finland. Kaarina succumbed to sepsis the following week.

In the weeks following Kaarina's death, Anya moved her effects to the Dunblane acreage and became Billy's full time caregiver. Her late husband

-- the scion of a wealthy farming family -- had been killed while serving in the U.S. army during the last days of the Great War.

Mourning the loss of her husband and her only sister and without children of her own, Anya gave all of her love and attention to her nephew. She came to dote on Billy, keeping the local post office, and the T.Eaton company mail order house in Winnipeg, busy with a stream of parcels containing toys, clothing and books for the boy.

Like her younger sister Anya was a teacher by profession and she supplemented Billy's grade school education with learning aids such as wall maps, encyclopedias, nature hikes and reading lists. She was particularly interested in building the boy's vocabulary and refining his manner of speech.

Anya kept the boy's parents alive in his memory by relating anecdotes of their lives in the Dakotas. She also told him of his uncle, Mingo Perala, who had fought in the Great War and won a medal for bravery and Toivo, his half-brother, who had enlisted in the Finnish army. Billy never tired of asking about his heritage and Anya complied with a vivid picture of Finnish-American and Finnish-Canadian lumberjacks, farmers and cowboys.

Billy had been an indifferent student prior to his aunt's arrival but now, because of her influence and passion for learning, he became a star pupil in the one-room country schoolhouse that he attended. During the school term, Anya would wait at the window for him to show up on Buster, the gelding she had purchased for him. She would have one of his favourite foods ready to serve and, over dinner, he would recount his day for her.

Their life was predictable, comfortable and insular and remained so for the better part of three years. Then, an agent of change appeared at their door in the person of Gus Holman, a short, heavy-set man who claimed to be an old friend of the family from North Dakota. When told of Vaiko's death Gus had reeled and reached out to a doorknob for support. At the news of Kaarina's fate, he broke down and cried. Touched by his compassion, Anya, who had left Gackle as a young bride, had lived in Bismarck for most of her adult life and didn't find it unusual that she had no previous knowledge of this visitor who claimed such close ties to her sister and her brother-in-law.

Gus found work in the CNR roundhouse in Dunblane and took lodgings in town although he spent most of his spare time at the acreage. He spent many hours working around the property, repairing and painting the house and outbuildings and demonstrating a puppy dog-like devotion to Anya. He would hang on her every word, springing to her side to open a door, bring her tea and generally preempt her from performing any task that she attempted.

An avid fan of boxing, Gus introduced Billy to the rudiments of the sport after the boy had come home from school with a black eye. At Gus's suggestion, Anya sent away for light and heavy punching bags, boxing gloves and a training helmet for the boy. Gus rigged up a ring in the hayloft of the old barn where he spent many hours working with the boy while Anya looked on.

Gus began spending so much time at the acreage that it made sense that he move into the house. Anya was an attractive woman -- who would have been described as zaftig (pleasingly plump) in certain cultures and full-figured in later times -- and it seemed natural when Gus's attentions advanced to nocturnal visits to her bed, where he patiently gave her pleasure. Soon they stood before a local Justice of the Peace, who performed the wedding ceremony. Billy, happy that his aunt and his friend were marrying, stood up as a witness.

After several months of marriage, Anya had remarked in a wistful tone, "You know. I miss going to town to pick up the mail and do some shopping. I'm getting fat sitting around here."

"But, Darling." Gus said. "That's what I'm here for. I'm in town everyday with the car and I can do everything that has to be done. And... you are not getting fat. You're still the best lookin' gal in the Coteau Hills. Tell you what. We'll have a party one a' these days so you can invite your friends from town."

She realized, at that moment, that she had no 'friends from town.' While it was true that she had a nodding acquaintance with some townspeople, the postmistress for one, she had not really connected with anyone. The party never materialized and she never pursued the issue.

When Anya mentioned that Billy needed a

space in which to do his school homework, Gus built an addition to the cottage, giving the boy a bright, sunlit room in which to study and keep his growing library and toy collection. When the renovation was complete, Anya presented the boy with a large globe of the planet, which took a place of prominence on a handsome oak desk that had recently arrived from Saskatoon. The room became known as Billy's study room.

One Friday afternoon in August, while Anya was sitting on the back steps drinking lemonade, and watching Billy as he unsaddled Buster, Gus appeared at the corner of the house in his customary oil-stained coveralls.

"I have some news," he grinned, eyes and teeth in sharp contrast to his grease-stained face.

"Oh," Anya looked up. "What is it, pray tell?"

"I got promoted."

"Well, congratulations are in order." She lifted her glass.

"Office job. No more dirty coveralls," he plucked at the collar of his oily garment.

"That will be good news for Sophie." Anya said. "The poor girl almost wears her hands off cleaning those things in kerosene."

Sophie was the teen-aged daughter of one of Gus's co-workers. He had cajoled Anya into hiring her on a part time basis but soon insinuated her into the household as live-in help. Sophie's job was to cook, fetch, carry, and clean the house. Gus made it clear to the girl that Anya was never to have a reason to exert herself. Billy liked Sophie and often helped her with her chores. He thought that one day he would marry her.

After his 'promotion,' Gus would leave the house each morning, dressed in a brightly striped shirt, gabardine trousers, two-toned wing tipped shoes and a straw boater, tipped rakishly over one eye. He would take Anya's Model T and depart for town.

Anya, who had a sweet tooth, continually gained weight on the rich fare prepared by Sophie and the sugary baked goods, which Gus brought from the bakery each day. She vowed to become more active and, against Gus's wishes, began attending Sunday services at the local Lutheran Church. One Sunday, Anya, Billy, Gus and Sophie, were sitting in the Model T preparing for a trip to church when Anya noticed that she had forgotten her hymnbook. Gus looked into the back seat and said: "Billy, go get your Aunt's book."

"No, no." Anya said, opening the front passenger door, "You sit still Honey. I'll get it. God knows. I need the exercise."

As Anya slowly made her way to the house, Billy realized how much weight she had gained in recent months. The week previous, she had taken a mysterious trip to Saskatoon; ostensibly to visit her lawyer, and returned in a somber mood. When Billy quizzed her about her health, she laughed it off, saying that she was as healthy as a horse.

When Anya didn't return to the car, Gus again turned to Billy. "Go get her. We're gonna be late." Billy, in a white suit and black patent leather shoes, ran in through the open front door and stopped in the hallway to admire himself in the mirror. Reflected in the glass behind him, he noticed a shoe protruding from behind the sitting room door. Turning and running to the doorway, he found Anya.

The boy existed in a daze following his aunt's death. Quiet by nature -- Anya had called him her little stoic – he had always been one to keep his emotions in check. He never cried upon incurring playtime injuries like bee stings or skinned knees and showed his happiness in quiet smiles. Because he was such an undemonstrative boy Anya showered him with things that she thought would make him happy. In actuality, he would have been more than happy in her care without the material gifts that she had bestowed upon him.

After the funeral, he spent the drive home crammed between Gus and Sophie on the front seat of the Model T. The backseat was covered with floral arrangements, which had been placed on the grave and later scooped up by Gus.

Parking on the gravel driveway, Gus turned off the engine and sat unmoving as Sophie exited the vehicle and made her way to the front door of the house. Uneasy at the hungry way Gus looked at the girl, Billy slid across the seat towards the open door. Before he was able to leave the car, Gus reached past him and pulled the door shut. Grabbing Billy by the arm, he hissed. "I don't want you in the house for an hour or so." Feeling that Gus was playing a joke on him, Billy attempted to break the grip on his arm. "I'm not shittin' ya," Gus said. "You stay outta the house for at least an hour or ... I promise you ... you'll be sorry."

"What do you mean?" Billy asked, growing nervous at the tightening pressure on his arm.

"I mean ..." Gus said, "that the good times are over for you little man. No more hidin' behind Anya's fat ass. Yer gonna start workin' fer yer keep from now on."

Shocked by Gus's ungallant description of his aunt, and frightened by the hostility of a man he had once considered to be a friend, Billy tried to pull his arm free. His tormenter's lips curled as he twisted the boy's arm backwards. "I'm ... not ... fuckin' ... kidding," he said in measured tones as Billy closed his eyes in pain.

"The gravy train stops here ya little shit ass." Gus punctuated his remarks by shoving Billy against the passenger door and opening his own.

As Gus made his way toward the house, Billy sat back against the seat, rubbing his arm while his mind reeled at the sudden turn of events. An ashen countenance, blinking eyes and ragged breathing reflected his emotional state and he opened his mouth and sucked in large draughts of air to forestall a feeling of nausea but he finally pushed the door open and vomited.

He warily circled the house before stepping on to the veranda and removing his shoes. Slowly opening the front door, he sidled into the entranceway, stopped and held his breath as he listened for a clue to Gus's whereabouts. He heard faint noises from the back of the house and padded down the hallway towards what had been Gus and Anya's bedroom. The door was closed, and the keyhole yielded nothing, but he became aware of a rhythmic squeaking sound emanating from inside the room. He slipped into his study room and emerged clutching his field glasses.

Making his way to the back of the property, to the structure that housed the sauna; he climbed up onto its roof and flattened himself on the shingles. He lifted the binoculars to his eyes and, after some adjustment, was afforded a view of the large window of the main bedroom. He aimed the glasses at the open window but was presented with only an expanse of whiteness. He turned the knob to sharpen the image and was surprised when a bare bottom popped into view. He felt his breathing tighten as he identified its owner.

Billy sharpened the image and saw Gus on the bed, his belly protruding from his open dress shirt. His mouth hung open and his eyes fluttered half-lidded as an unclothed Sophie straddled his lower body. Gus's arms were extended upward, his hands cupping her breasts. Sophie, whose head was thrown back allowing her unbound hair to stream down her back, moved languidly on her partner and appeared to be a more than willing participant in the affair. Billy lowered the binoculars and realized that his world had become a stranger, colder place.

Gus's good guy act had lasted until the funeral. During the ceremony he had appeared to be consumed with grief, tearfully acknowledging the mourners who lined up to pay their respects. During the period between Anya's death and the funeral, Gus had been distant to Billy but the boy assumed that it was due to the man's desolation at losing his wife.

That evening, at the supper table, Gus began to impose a new set of rules for the household. After the meal, which Sophie cooked, Billy was ordered to clean up. The boy was scandalized at the suggestion but soon realized what Gus meant business.

"From now on," Gus pronounced, "Sophie will have yer bedroom upstairs."

Billy nodded. "That's O.K. I can sleep in my study room." He had often coaxed Anya into allowing him to sleep in the room containing his toys and books, but she insisted that he have no distractions or diversions at bedtime and so made him sleep in his bedroom on the second floor.

"No, I'm takin' over yer study room. I'm puttin' in the heavy bag and some ring equipment and some tables where my buddies and I can play poker."

"Where do I sleep?"

"I'm settin' up an army cot in the kitchen. You'll sleep there. First thing in the morning your job will be to start a fire in the cook stove and get a pot a' coffee goin'."

Billy's heart fell at the news but he refused to show any emotion. He stood up to leave the table but Gus grabbed his arm, pulling him back into his chair. "Siddown. I ain't done with you yet. Sophie has to visit her folks once in awhile so I gave her yer horse. Any objections?" Gus sat smirking at him but Billy refused to give him the satisfaction of a protest. He shook his head.

"I'll clean my stuff out of the study room."

"Leave it where it is. Sophie's got her brothers and sisters comin' over to go through it. You can get started on the dishes now...we're done."

Billy stood and walked into the kitchen. He felt a weakness overtake him as his mind reeled at the recent turn of events. He immersed a dipper into the stove's reservoir and poured hot water into the galvanized iron sink. Then he added some powdered soap and then used the cistern pump to add cold water so he could immerse his hands and wash the dishes. When he returned to the dining room to collect the soiled tableware, Gus and Sophie were gone. The sound of singing bedsprings found their way to the kitchen and Billy shut his eyes tightly. A warm tear coursed down his cheek.

"You son-of-a bitching bastard," he whispered.

Over the ensuing months, Gus seemed to revel in making Billy's life miserable. Anything the boy favoured was taken from him and any onerous chore, which Gus could devise, fell to Billy. Finally Sophie tired of Gus, and his treatment of the boy, and retreated to her home. She resisted all of Gus's entreaties to return and, eventually ran off with a dry goods salesman.

After Sophie's departure, Gus began to spend more time in town and Billy was happy at the freedom afforded him although Gus would show up with job lists for him and appear periodically to check on his progress.

Then one day in 1927...it all changed.

"Hey you. Boy! Wake up."

The sound of a deep male voice startled Billy into wakefulness. He pushed back his baseball cap and sat up on the stone boat where he had been napping. He had spent the morning selecting and loading fieldstones onto the primitive vehicle for a projected stone fence that Gus was planning near the main house.

Buster, who had strained to pull one loaded sledge up the hill that morning, remained hitched to the conveyance and now stood head down several feet away. A tall man, whose face was shadowed by a wide brimmed hat, stood examining the horse.

"You tryin' to kill this feller?"

Billy shook his head and stared at a tall, slim man -- with a cowboy moustache on his upper lip -- in the vest and trousers of a pinstriped business suit over an open-collared white dress shirt. A silver watch chain ran from one vest pocket, through a buttonhole and into the opposite pocket. The man's pants legs were tucked into a pair of high-cut Mexican riding boots and his hat was a silver-grey Stetson with a Concho hatband and a Carlsbad crease in the crown.

"Is this yore horse?" The man said.

"N-no. Well...he used to be my horse until Gus gave him to Sophie. After she ran off, her dad wouldn't give the horse back, so Gus beat up on him and took Buster back. Buster stepped on Gus's foot, so he told me I wasn't supposed to water him until I was finished for the day."

"That son of a bitch... if this horse doesn't get some water soon there's gonna be a dead animal on the place. Lend a hand. Unhook them traces and git some water into that trough up there. This pore old boy needs help fast. Christ! It's hotter than hell out here. It must be in the high eighties.

"O.K. Buster, let's get this tack offa ya," the man's voice was soothing as he removed the bit from the horse's mouth and unfastened the bridle from around the animal's head.

Billy unhitched the traces from the stone boat and threw them over Buster's back. Then he ran to the well and began pumping water into the trough. The stranger led Buster to the water, removed his harness and collar and threw them to the ground. The horse, which had been treated badly during the past months, had developed an ill temper but didn't show any animosity to the cowboy, nuzzling him before lowering his nose to the water. The man let the big animal drink for several moments and then pulled him back and walked him slowly around the barnyard. The cowboy turned to Billy.

"Scare up some gunny sacks, willya, kid?"

Billy nodded and made for the root cellar adjacent to the house. He pulled open one of its horizontally mounted doors, allowing it to fall open, and ran down a series of wooden steps into the musty coolness of the underground chamber. A bin holding potatoes and root vegetables yielded a number of burlap gunnysacks and Billy ran back up the stairs bearing an armful.

As he made his way downhill he assessed the stranger. Standing next to the cowboy Billy had felt insignificant in his torn denim overalls, weathered ball cap and ragged canvas running shoes. His blonde, almost white, hair had been uncut for months and now reached his shoulders. His face and hands were covered with a film of dust and sweat.

"Well...don't just stand there Squirt. Start wiping him down. Git all that foamy sweat offa him so we can let him cool out in the barn."

When Billy completed the wipe down, the man put a hand on Buster's neck and guided the horse toward the barn. "Run ahead and get some chop into a nose bag, willya?" Billy nodded and ran into the coolness of the barn where he scooped some of the oaten mixture into a nosebag and handed it to the man, who fastened it over Buster's mouth.

"What you doin' with all them rocks?"

"Gus is planning to build a fieldstone fence around the house. He saw one in Saskatoon and decided he should have one just like it."

"And, how long you bin doin' this...haulin' these stones?"

"A week... and a couple days."

"Jesus H. Christ! A few more days a' this and you'd have killed ole Buster fer sure. Just where the hell is Gus anyway?"

"He's either in the pool hall or the beer parlour."

"Doesn't he work fer a livin'?"

"He used to work in the roundhouse but he claimed that he got a promotion. Every morning, he dressed up like a slick and went to town. Sophie told me that he didn't get a promotion. He was fired. Sophie also told me that Gus had studied up on Anya when he was back in North Dakota. He knew that she was a rich widow with a bad heart so he did his best to make it worse. He told Sophie that, after Anya died, the place would be his and they could get married. Sophie didn't like him, but she said it was better than living at home. First chance she got, she left town.

Now that he's got Auntie Anya's money Gus plays pool or sits in the beer parlour. He doesn't do any work around here, cause he says I have to earn my keep."

"And, what does 'earning your keep' mean?"

"Well, I load rocks, I collect the eggs and milk the cow. I clean up after meals. And, I sweep the floors and cook supper."

"What did this Sophie do around here?"

"She was our hired girl... until Auntie Anya died. Then she was Gus's girlfriend."

"Did Sophie live in the house while Anya was there?"

"Yep."

"That dirty little son of a bitch." Mingo brushed dust from his vest. "I've worked up a thirst. You got anything around here in the way of a cold drink?"

"There's beer. Gus keeps some bottles in a pail

in the well. There's root beer too... but Gus would raise heck if I took some... he counts the bottles."

"Well, Mister Billy Jurva." the man smiled. "Gus Holman is through countin' bottles around here."

"How come you know my name?"

"I know a lot about you."

"Are you Mingo?"

"That's what they call me."

"Auntie Anya said that you would come for me someday."

"I knew you were in good hands with Anya...I'm real sorry I didn't come here as soon as I found out about her passing away but the state of Montana needed my help in building some roads."

"Roads?" The boy's eyes brightened. "Did you use a Fresno?"

"I have been known to use a Fresno. But, most a' the time I just used a pick and shovel or sometimes a post maul like the rest of the road builders."

"Why did you go there?"

"Well now. That's a long story Bill. When we have some time, I'll tell you all about it. Mingo glanced toward the road leading to the house. What kind of car does Gus drive?"

"He drives Auntie Anya's Model T. That's him comin' now."

"Well, that's good. That means I won't haveta go and drag him outta the beer parlour."

"Billy said: "Looks like I'm going to catch it though."

Mingo turned to his nephew and placed a

crooked forefinger under his chin. "Gus is through bossing you around. I wasn't kidding about that."

"How do you know that?"

"Trust me."

"Then whose place is it?"

"You'll soon find out." Mingo chuckled.

"Gus is tough. He's beat up on a lot of guys."

"We'll see how tough he is." Mingo smiled.

They watched as the Model T -- followed by a large dust plume -- turned into the yard in front of the house. A heavy set, red-faced man hopped out and made for the barn where Billy and Mingo stood. The man wore a green and white striped shirt and tan gabardine slacks. He spit out the stub of a cigar, mashed it with a two-toned wingtip, pushed his straw boater off of his forehead and approached them.

"Bill. You git up to the house... I'll deal 'th you later." He turned to Mingo. "I don't know who in hell you are fella, but I'll ask you to leave my proppity. Now..." he clapped his hands, "Toot Sweet."

Billy made a move to comply but Mingo restrained him with a hand on his shoulder.

"You use the term 'proppity' a little loosely there Fatso. I'm here to represent the legal owner of this property and see that you get th' hell off of it."

Gus took a step backward in surprise. "Why that's bullshit. My wife was the legal owner a' this place. When she died, it passed to me."

"This place never belonged to Anya." Mingo said. "It is still registered to the Jurva family. You bin tryin' to finagle this here boy outta his rightful inheritance."

"That don't make no difference. No how. I'm also the' legal guardian of this here boy. So clear off my proppity." Gus's voice rose.

Mingo produced a document from an inside pocket of his vest.

"That's not what Anya's will says."

"Anya's will?"

"You didn't know she wrote a will, didya? She filed it with the public trustee in Regina and sent a copy to me." He handed the paper to Gus. "Read it."

Gus unfolded the document and spent several moments with it. Then he tore it into shreds, threw it into the air, and laughed. "So much for that."

"Jesus, Gus. You think that one was the only copy?"

Gus's gaze fell to the shreds of paper at his feet for several moments before he looked up. "Well, possession is nine-tenths a' th' law. I'm in possession a' this place as the heir of my dead wife."

"I'll say this fer ya. You are one hard-headed son of a bitch," Mingo said, pulling a folded envelope from a pants pocket. He fished in his shirt for a pair of steel-rimmed glasses and, perching them on his nose, removed a letter from the envelope and began to read.

Dearest Mikko,
I have been to see a doctor in Saskatoon and he tells me that my heart is in bad

repair. It appears that I have the same condition that Mother had.

I am terrified of what will become of Billy if something happens to me. I do not trust Gus to look after him; he will pursue his own selfish interests to the detriment of the boy.

I am aware of your present situation and realize that you are not free to travel. But, I trust that you will soon be free to come here and I hope that I will survive to see that day. It has been an eternity since I have set eyes on you.

Billy has been such a blessing to me. Since poor Kaarina died, he is, in all things, my own son.

In the event that something should happen to me before you arrive, I am enclosing a copy of my will. You will note that Gus will receive no proceeds from my estate for reasons I will explain.

In recent months I have been in correspondence with a woman from North Dakota who claims to be Gus's legal wife. She sent me a photo reproduction of their marriage certificate and swears that they were never divorced. It seems that Gus may even have another wife in the old country. When I broached the subject with him, He blew up. He claimed he was being victimized in a con job...

Gus uttered a guttural sound, put his head down and charged at Mingo. The big cowboy calmly pushed Billy out of harm's way and, stepping back, extended a boot, tripping Gus and causing him to leave his feet and land heavily several feet away. He regained his feet, pulled his straw hat down and reached into a back pocket of his trousers.

"He's got a knuckle duster." Billy warned.

Mingo removed his glasses, folded them and tucked them into a shirt pocket and waited for Gus, who had applied a set of brass knuckles to his right hand and was advancing with a smirk on his face.

"I've had a belly full a' you, you sorry son of a bitch." Mingo grabbed Gus by his collar and held him at arm's length preventing the man's shorter arms from landing a punch. He batted Gus's hat off with his free hand and buried his fingers in the man's pomaded hair, pulling his head down smartly and kneeing him in the face. He followed up with a kick to the man's groin.

Gus slumped to the ground and curled into a ball. As Mingo approached him, he held up a hand in surrender. Mingo gestured for the brass knuckles and Gus flipped them off of his hand and unto the ground at Billy's feet. The boy -- awestruck by his uncle's cool efficiency -- picked them up and pocketed them.

"Enough Mingo. Enough." Blood flowed from Gus's mouth and both nostrils and he rolled back and forth not knowing what pain to address.

"So... you know who I am." Mingo said, removing

a folded bandanna from a rear pants pocket and dropping it on Gus's shoulder.

"Yah, yah. You're Anya'th brother. Th' famuth war hero." His voice was muffled by the handkerchief, which he held to his nose to staunch the blood flow.

"Nonammit," he snuffled, lifting a bare knee, which protruded from a rent in his slacks. "You tore my new panth."

"You tore yer own pants," Mingo said and pulled out his pocket watch. "It's now 12:45 on the clock Gus. I'm givin' you one hour to collect yer kit and hit the road."

"I ain't goin' nowhere. Thith here'th my place. I put a lot of dough into fixin' it up."

"That's rich." Fer ever' dollar you put in, you took two out of Anya's bank account. Do you know there's a warrant out on you on both sides a' the border? Yer wanted fer for bigamy and embezzlement. The wife that you jumped ship on in North Dakota is in Saskatoon lookin' to collect a piss pot full of cash she says you stole from her. Plus, she's got a couple of gorillas traveling with her. Goons I sure as hell wouldn't want to tangle with."

"Aw snit," Gus said, scrambling to his feet. "She brought her brotherth." He made for the house and soon was seen shoving a suitcase into the Model T and speeding away.

"But, that's Auntie Anya's car." Billy said.

"Don't worry. I got some people who will bring it back."

"Is Gus's real wife in Saskatoon?"

"Nah," Mingo gave a rumbling chuckle. She's right here in Dunblane. With a lawyer and two of her gangster brothers."

Several hours after Gus had departed, a long black Packard sedan followed by Anya's Model T pulled up to the house. A woman exited the Packard from the driver's side and approached the big cowboy who had stepped up to meet her. Billy was surprised when they embraced and kissed.

"Are you leaving?" Billy said.

Before his uncle could reply the woman reached out and pulled the boy to her "You must be Billy. The boy I've heard so much about." She spoke in what Billy took to be an English accent. "We'll have to clean you up so they will let you on the train."

"Train?" Billy said, his eyes growing wide.

"Yes." The woman said. "Hasn't your uncle spoken to you about your relocation to Edmonton?"

Mingo grinned and turned to his nephew. "Moira is looking to buy your place. She wants to build a hall for those Red Finns she hangs around with." He ducked back as Moira aimed a playful slap at him.

"I don't hang around with those Red Finns. I help organize them like I organize a lot of poor people who get hurt by the system. This place will be perfect... that's if it's alright with you Billy."

Billy stood wide-eyed. "What place are you talking about?"

"Why," Moira said. "This place." She waved around her around her. "Your place."

"This is my place?"

"It shore is partner." Mingo said. "Lock stock and storm windows. Anya kept up th' taxes but your dad paid cash for this property in 1911 and the title never left your family."

Two men in business suits exited the Model T and joined the group around Billy.

"These likely looking lads are my lawyers. Reginald Goodkey and Martin Theuss." Moira said. "We have been in Regina to defend some strikers who were imprisoned over some nasty business at a mine. And... also in Montana to bail out a naughty cowboy."

Mingo had entered Montana to collect some money from a former associate only to discover that there was an arrest warrant out for him in the state. He was taken into custody and spent several months on a road gang before Moira and her lawyers arrived to spring him. Freddie Hafner -- who claimed that Mingo had killed his brother Erwin -- had sworn out the complaint but was highly embarrassed when Mingo's defence team produced Erwin Hafner in the courtroom. All charges had been dropped and Freddie was taken into custody.

At first Billy had been unnerved by the appearance of the well-dressed strangers because he thought that they had 'orphanage' written all over them. In the funny papers, Little Orphan Annie was always up against bad people from orphanages and he thought he was in for it because he belonged in that category. He relaxed visibly when he discovered that his visitors proved to have his best interests at heart and began to cope with the fact that the house -- in which he had been a virtual servant -- actually belonged to him. He tugged at his uncle's vest,

"Uncle Mingo, what would I do in Edmonton?"

"Well, Nephew Billy. "Fer openers, you can help me with my horses..."

"Or," Moira interjected. "You come with me to Montreal. I have a son about your age. We would love to have you."

"What about Buster?"

"Buster is going to Edmonton. He needs to rest up and fill his belly with oats. There's a feller I know in Dunblane who will take the cow and chickens of yer hands."

"I want to go with you and Buster." Billy said and, turning to Moira. "Sorry. You can have the house though."

"That's all right Love. I understand. Now, let's get your hair cut, get you a bath, and find you something to wear on the train."

Most of Billy's good clothing had been given to Sophie's brothers and he had grown out of the garments that remained so Moira took the situation in hand. "Mingo, you and the boys, she nodded at Goodkey and Theuss, square up things around here. I'm taking Billy into town. The little chap can't go anywhere in the rags he's wearing."

Billy was impressed with Moira's take-charge attitude and her ability to maneuver the big Packard around the ruts and stones of the dirt road that lead to town. Once there, she marched him into the barber shop and approached the barber.

"Good afternoon my good man. I have a tumbleweed here that needs some trimming." The man put down his copy of the Star-Phoenix and rose. "Now, just a minute there, lady. This boy's dirty. He probbly has cooties."

"You find cooties on this little chap and I'll give you a nickel for each one you find. He's been working out on the range. He's just got a little trail dust on him. That's all. " She winked at Billy.

"That's a deal," the barber said and placed a board across the arms of the ornate barber chair. He lifted Billy onto it, removed the headrest and, with a foot pedal, elevated the chair until Billy's head was at the right level. He fastened a barber's cape around the boy and began combing out his tangled locks. Moira sat down and picked up the barber's newspaper.

The sights, sounds and smells of the place, impressed Billy, who had never been in a barbershop. He sat quietly while the man began snipping off hanks of hair, which slid down the cape to the floor. As he submitted to the barber's ministrations, he decided that he liked Moira and her range and tumbleweed references. She made it sound like he was a real cowboy even if he didn't look like one.

After the barber finished up by trimming Billy's neck with a straight razor, he held a hand mirror to the boy's head to allow him to see the back of his head in the wall mirror. "You care for some hair tonic sir?" Billy looked to Moira and she smiled and nodded. The man reached to a shelf behind him and picked up a bottle with a rubber nozzle. He shook out a gelatinous mixture, which he rubbed into the boy's hair. Billy watched in the wall mirror as the man combed his newly shorn locks into a pompadour.

"Well, what d'ya think young fella?"

Billy smiled and nodded his approval and the man removed the cloth cape and placed the boy on the floor. "Well missus. I didn't find no cooties so, you just owe me fifteen cents. He's a good boy. He don't jump around and carry on like a lot of 'em do."

"He is a good boy, isn't he? Moira removed a fifty-cent coin from her purse and handed it to the man.

"Just a minute, ma'am. I'll get you yer change."

"No change necessary. You are a good sport. Some barbers wouldn't have touched this little chap in his present condition."

The barber beamed at the compliment. "Next time this little fella needs a haircut it's on the house."

"Why, that is so kind. But Billy here is going back to the ranch tomorrow."

From the barbershop, Moira took him into the dry goods store and, after asking the shopkeeper what boys his age were wearing, had him outfitted with a checkered shirt, a pair of GWG bib overalls and several pairs of summer underwear. She found him a pair of ankle height leather shoes and added several pairs of socks. The clerk wrapped everything in a brown paper parcel, which he handed to the boy. Billy didn't have the heart to tell her that she had outfitted him like a farmer. Not like a cowboy.

From the dry goods store they proceeded to the hotel where Moira negotiated a bath for her new friend. When Billy was immersed in a sea of bubbles, she entered and scrubbed him with a sponge, being careful not to cause the boy any embarrassment. In Billy's eyes, anything Moira could have done would have been O.K., after her cowboy remarks.

As they sat down on a bench on main street, eating ice cream cones, Moira turned to her well-scrubbed, well-dressed companion and said: "I have noticed the way you take in the sights of this town. Didn't you come here often?"

"I've never been here before."

"No one ever brought you to town? Not even Anya?"

"No. Auntie Anya used to come to town when I was in school. She'd pick up parcels at the post office so she could surprise me when I got home. Then Gus showed up and Auntie didn't go to town anymore."

"Well, enough said about that low-life bastard. He's in a jail cell where he belongs. " Moira grasped Billy's arm. "Please pardon my bad language dear."

"That's O.K.," Billy said. "He is a low-life bastard."

Moira hooted with laughter and hugged the boy. Let's finish these cones and get back to the house and get you squared away for your train trip tomorrow."

The next morning, Billy donned his new garments and took a last walk around the only home he had ever known. It had been a scene of happiness and despair and -- for the latter reason -- he felt no qualms about leaving it. The next morning, after a visit to Kaarina and Anya's graves, Moira delivered Billy and Mingo to the railway station.

Moira and Mingo had a moment together and Billy heard her say: "I'll have the papers for your guardianship of Billy ready when I see you next week." Then she approached Billy, gave him a hug, and said, "See you soon. Cowboy."

Sitting at the window of the passenger coach, Billy wished that the train ride would last forever. He leaned out the open window of the car and, even though he received an occasional gust of smoke and cinders, he happily inhaled the smells of rail travel.

After Anya's death, he had often lain awake, on his cot in the kitchen, listening to the whistle of a train moving across the prairie. He would picture the passengers -- as they often appeared in Anya's magazines -- dressed to the nines and sitting in the dining car being served by white-jacketed waiters while en route to exciting destinations. Now his dream had come true. His turn had finally come.

"Lookit all them fences Bill," Mingo said from

the facing seat, interrupting Billy's reverie. "Sod busters. They put their danged bob wire across open range, and cowboys ... like you and me? Well, we just can't ride the range no more. This is short grass country. Buffalo range. It goes all the way to Calgary and it should only be used to graze cattle."

"How about the buffalo. Where are they?" Billy's eyes lit up at the prospect of seeing some of the legendary beasts.

"Stuffed and in museums. Back in the old days, the guvamint kilt off the buffalo, starved out the Indins, and opened up th' land fer farmers. The farmers plowed up the topsoil and watched the wind blow it away into Alberta. This has got to be some of the toughest land in the world to farm. If it ain't hoppers, its hail. If it ain't hail, its drought, or early frost. If those don't git ya, then the banker surely will."

"Are the Indians in museums too?"

"No, they're still around. The guvamint tried to turn them into farmers. Fer the most part, it didn't work. They're good horsemen and they love to rodeo and race but most of 'em aren't happy followin' a plow." Mingo looked at his nephew in his bib overalls and checkered shirt.

"When we get to Saskatoon, we'll have to get you into proper kit. You look like a plow-jockey in them duds."

The train from Dunblane to Saskatoon had been a freight train with a passenger coach at the tail end but to Billy it felt like a sleek transcontinental train.

In Saskatoon they checked into the newly built Bessborough Hotel and, after a meal in the hotel dining room, Mingo took Billy to a store and had him outfitted him in cowboy gear; a wide-brimmed cowboy hat, the smallest riding boots the store had in stock, several pairs of denim trousers and three cowboy shirts. Billy wore his new cowboy gear out of the store and reveled in the smiles of onlookers as he accompanied his uncle to the hotel, where they deposited the parcel containing Billy's farmer clothes and continued on to a movie theatre where they saw Tom Mix in *Riders of the Purple Sage.*

Billy was enthralled by his first movie and imagined riding alongside the train as it travelled westward through miles of unchanging landscape. It was a long expanse of prairie called 'The Big Lonely' by hobos who rode the rails across it. The rhythmic click of the rails eventually caused Billy's eyes to close and he fell asleep propped up against the window of the coach. Mingo rearranged him on the seat and covered him with a blanket while the boy slept through the night, waking as the train passed through the hamlet of Millet Alberta. He read the name on a series of grain elevators as they glided past.

"Millet? Where is that?"

"Millet is almost home. We'll be in Edmonton in no time. First. Let's go see what kinda grub they're serving in the dining car."

When they detrained in Edmonton, Mingo led

Billy out of the station and pointed him to an Essex sedan, which was pulling up to the curb in front of them. Mingo threw his bag into the backseat and pulled open the passenger door for Billy who slid onto the front seat to find himself sitting next to the most beautiful woman he had ever seen.

"Hi Billy," she said, extending her hand to him. "I'm Faith."

Billy felt something akin to a mild electric shock at the touch of her hand and he didn't relinquish it until Mingo said: "She's gonna need both hands to drive Partner."

Flushing a bright hue of pink, Billy dropped her hand and sat back, mortified at his gaffe.

"It's O.K. Billy," Faith squeezed his shoulder. I'll hold hands with you any time."

Billy's face took on an even brighter hue as Faith nosed the Essex onto the street, and merged into the traffic on Jasper Avenue. The volume and the speed of traffic soon replaced his feeling of discomfort with one of trepidation. Automobiles seemed to be coming at them from all directions and streetcars, like railway coaches that had broken away from a train, seemed to be arbitrarily careering down city thoroughfares. Only his innate stoicism prevented him from crying out in concern.

It wasn't until he realized that the traffic lights -- which looked like green, yellow and red candies -- regulated the traffic and prevented motorists from engaging in one collective collision.

Faith turned onto a street and proceeded north

for a time, until they came to level crossing with a long freight train making for it.

"Dammit... but that's a long drag. We're going to be here all day." Faith said and impulsively floored the gas pedal causing the car to leap forward toward the crossing and reaching it scant seconds ahead of the freight, now voicing its anger with a series of shrill whistle blasts. The Essex Super Six rocketed across the tracks and proceeded north. Face flushed and with eyes sparkling, Faith turned to Billy. "Did that get your blood rushing Billy?"

Nodding solemnly, Billy relaxed his arms after having pushed them strenuously against the car's dashboard.

"Now that!" Mingo said, "is why Ewan doesn't like you drivin'."

"Oh, I know. I get a little reckless sometimes."

"A little reckless?" Mingo said. "You got the guts of a bugler."

Coming from a bare prairie landscape, Billy was awestruck by the number of trees that bordered the lane leading to the Fraser house. Faith had rolled down her window and the fragrance of the forest wafted into the car as it approached a well-kept two-storey residence.

"We'll have lunch," she announced, turning to Mingo. "Then you and Billy can check on your horses. Deke's has been over there every day but he was saying something about going fishing on the Sturgeon today. Any way, he'll be home for supper, and then you boys can get acquainted.

Chapter 2 - Derek Fraser

Riviere Qui Barre Alberta, July 1919

"For the last time! I don't want him." The young woman said as she folded a dress and placed it into a cardboard suitcase.

"But he is your child," an older woman said.

"He's not my child. He's the child of that bastard rapist, Callum Fraser."

"Shh. Do not speak ill of the dead." The older woman said, holding a forefinger to her lips.

"I would piss on his grave. If I knew where it was," the girl said as she wrapped a kerchief around her hair. "Keep him or give him to the nuns." She embraced her mother, picked up her suitcase and left the room.

The woman watched as the girl seated herself beside the driver of a black Ford sedan and lifted a hand to her mother as the car departed the farmyard and made for the highway. When the car was no longer visible, the older woman retreated into the house to address the needs of a crying baby.

❁   ❁   ❁

Edmonton Alberta – January 1924

"Hey, Papoose. I heard Pa say he's gonna kick you guys out tonight. You'll be a little frozen potato in the morning"

The boy, to whom the remarks were directed, turned and stared at his companion. He felt blood leave his face and, fighting back an urge to vomit, ran from the room.

It had happened again. He and his uncle had once again become unwanted guests, as they had in different households where they had lived. In each case, his uncle's freeloading ways and refusal to work for a living had resulted in their exile. On many occasions, their hosts would ask that the boy be left in their care but he was a meal ticket that his uncle would not relinquish.

Now, a tense situation had developed between his uncle and Andrew Melnyk, the man of the house. The boy was terrified that he and his uncle would be turned out into the subzero January weather that had enveloped the area over the past week. He, who had known a loving, comfortable life in the home of his grandmother, now endured an unsettled existence in the care of his uncle.

The boy's life had changed dramatically on a September day in 1923 after he and his grandmother attended a birthday celebration at a relative's farm. Music made with fiddles, spoons, drums, accordions, pianos and other implements and instruments made the party memorable for the boy. Two female cousins took him in tow and conducted him around to members of his extended family. His relatives filled his pockets with candies and introduced him to foods and sweets that were new to him.

The following morning he rode home in front of his grandmother on her saddle horse Ginger. A mile into their journey, they encountered a man carrying a .22 rifle accompanied by three mangy looking dogs. When the animals spotted Ginger they made for her and began nipping at her heels, causing the horse to rear up and unseat her riders. The boy's grandmother instinctively wrapped her arms around the child and provided him with a soft landing. When she fell to the ground her head snapped back and struck a large stone on the gravel road.

Following the loss of his grandmother, the boy's uncle August became his guardian. The boy and his uncle lived with a succession of relatives and friends until August brought the boy to Edmonton to the household of cousin Clothilde Melnyk. Clothilde, her husband Andrew and three children, lived in a small house near the Calder marshalling yard where Andrew was employed as a switchman.

Soon after their arrival Andrew found August a job as a car checker in the rail yard. August worked two shifts and quit, citing an 'inability to work with idiots.' Andrew, a man who was well regarded in the community, found him other jobs but August would quit on the first or second day because his co-workers failed to measure up to his standards. He preferred to stay in the warm house, making conversation with his cousin over cigarettes and coffee. Andrew was an even-tempered man but August's actions eventually drove him to deliver an ultimatum. "Find a job or find another place to live."

Often, when Andrew was absent on a four to midnight shift, August would sit for hours at the dinner table bemoaning the fact that Métis people with his credentials were not accepted as the equals of white men. At other times he would regale the family about the great horse culture of the Prairies.

"Our people were buffalo hunters. We were the great Métis horsemen who rode the open prairie. We built an empire that was bigger than the whole Roman Empire put together and we had our own government in Fort Garry, led by Louis Riel and Gabriel Dumont. Then the CPR came through and cheated we plainsmen of our lands and our way of life. That dirty bastard John A. Macdonald and his government bribed witnesses and then hung Riel for treason."

"Language, August." Clothilde cautioned.

"Did you ride with Riel? One of Clothilde's daughters asked.

"I was too young." August said. "But my granddad and his brothers rode with Dumont."

Educated at a Catholic seminary, where he

had excelled in languages and the arts, August had been his family's bright light. His father, who died when August was in his teens, thought his son was destined for the priesthood. His mother held out hope that he would become a teacher. Unfortunately, neither objective was realized, as August subscribed to the belief that he was of a special breed; a man destined for great things, not a man who could waste his time performing menial labour. He was, he believed, born in the wrong place at the wrong time. He considered himself a Renaissance man, someone who belonged in 17th century Florence rather than 20thcentury Edmonton.

His mother had bequeathed a portion of her estate to August, specifically earmarked for her grandson. The money, administered by an Edmonton law firm, was allocated for the boy's care and education but August's freeloading ways and his ability to generate phoney invoices allowed him to divert a good part of it to his own bank account. He was accumulating a stake; money that would allow him to pursue a career path that became apparent to him one evening in an Edmonton movie theatre.

For sometime, some years before his sister had given birth to the boy, August had followed the career of the actor Rudolph Valentino and became convinced that he could succeed in an atmosphere where a man like Valentino had become a great star.

His mother's death, and her bequest, made

his dreams a reality and, after two years, he had saved enough money to finance his escape to a new lifestyle in California. He had accumulated enough money for train fare and living expenses and most importantly, dancing lessons, as the tango appeared to be the dance of choice for Latin Lovers on the silver screen.

As August was holding forth at the dinner table one evening, Andrew entered. He came in stamping the snow off of his boots and rubbing frost from his eyebrows. He approached the table and pounded it with a mitted hand, causing August's plate to bounce.

"You son of a bitch!" Andrew hissed. "I just found out you have money in the bank and here you' bin freeloading' offa us for a year and haven't thrown in one bloody red cent."

"You have no way of knowing how much I have in the bank." August said. "The fact is... I don't even have a bank account."

"Oh Christ. Spare me the bullshit. You have four hundred in the Imperial Bank."

"That is false! August said, half rising from his seat and pointing a finger at Andrew. "I'll have whoever told you that... fired."

"If you want to be run out of town on a rail you will. I want you outta this house by noon tomorrow. The boy stays here with us."

"But, Andrew." Clothilde protested. "Where will August go in this weather?"

"Christ. With his money he can stay at the bloody Macdonald Hotel. I gotta get back to work.

But... what I said stands," Andrew pointed a finger at August.

"Tomorrow. Noon."

After Andrew had departed, August rose from the table. "Well, I guess that means we better get going."

"You can't go tonight. It's 30 below out there. And what do you mean 'we better get going?'" Clothilde said.

"The kid and I." He said, pointing at the boy. Can you get him dressed for the weather?"

"But, he doesn't have any warm clothes." Clothilde said, tears in her eyes. "Go... if you must, but please leave the little fellow here with us."

"I am his legal guardian and he goes where I go. Maybe he can borrow some of Melvin's winter clothes?"

"Hey, I need my clothes." Melvin said. "But he can have the stuff that don't fit me no more."

August wrinkled his brow and frowned, "Doesn't fit me anymore. Really Melvin, that is a double negative." Ever the pedant, August shook his head at the boy.

During the exchange, the boy sat rigid and speechless. He knew that the moment of his demise -- the moment that Melvin had predicted -- had arrived. He was about to perish in the cold.

When August and the boy were ready to leave, Clothilde took up a position by the door.

"I am not letting you take this boy out of this house."

"Hildy." August soothed, using a pet name. "We

are just going two blocks from the streetcar. I will follow Andrew's advice and book a hotel room."

Several hours later, the boy sat on a kitchen chair, shivering beside a Quebec heater. August had dragged him through a subzero snowstorm -- cursing at him when his short legs weren't able to keep the pace -- and finally picking the boy up and carrying him to a two-storey brick farmhouse tucked into a wooded clearing.

August had done some research on Callum Fraser, the man fingered by his sister as the father of the boy. He knew that she had fallen in with a rough crowd in Edmonton and Fraser was probably some drifter with whom she had a fling. But, he had recently been told of a well-to-do family named Fraser, who had a residence north of the city. Andrew's ultimatum had forced him to put his game plan into action sooner than he had planned; he would spend the night in a hotel, maybe not the Macdonald, but something downtown. Tomorrow he would buy some appropriate clothing and catch a train to the coast.

The only loose end was the kid. The money would go a lot farther if he ditched the little bugger. He should have left him with Clothilde but he perversely wanted her to feel bad about the situation. He had decided to take a long shot and simply leave the kid with the Fraser family. Chances were good that they would take him in and keep him warm. A thought crossed his mind that he might be missing an opportunity for a finder's fee, or a little graft; if they were the right Frasers.

But, California beckoned and he decided to ditch the kid on their front porch and high tail it for fame and fortune.

As they approached a white-painted veranda, August lifted the boy, carried him up the steps and dropped him in front of the entrance door. He shoved a folded piece of paper at him and said. "Give them this." He turned, pounded on the door with the heel of his hand, and disappeared into the snowstorm.

The boy stood at the door, terrified that no one would answer his uncle's summons and also terrified that someone would. He was about to turn and pursue August, when the door opened and a tall black-haired man, with a briar pipe clenched in his teeth, emerged from the house. The man looked blankly at the small figure for a moment, then noting the second set of footprints, walked onto the veranda and peered into the falling snow. Shaking his head, he scooped up the boy, pulled the door shut, and deposited him in the warm confines of a kitchen redolent of pipe tobacco.

Helping to unwrap a frost-rimed scarf from the boy's face the man said, "What's your name boy?" The boy, who wore an adult sized tweed jacket over a Cowichan sweater and woolen trousers and high-top rubber boots, pushed a toque off of his forehead and stuttered. "D-Deke. I-I'm f-five years old."

An older version of the man with the pipe entered the room.

"Wot tha hell is goin' on Ewan?"

"It appears that we have an orphan of the

storm Malcolm. This little fella was just left on our doorstep with a letter in his hand." Ewan unfolded the page of lined foolscap and began to read.

To the Fraser family,

The boy standing before you is of your blood. He is your grandson and the issue of a union between your late son Callum Fraser and my sister Yvette, who has expressed no interest in caring for her offspring.

Due to an inexplicable bias against me here in Edmonton, I am relocating to a friendlier environment but, alas, I cannot take the lad with me.

The boy appears to have some speech difficulties in that he hardly ever says a word. In any case, his name is Derek but apparently he prefers the name Deke.

Sincerely
August Ouellette.

"Some son ay a hoor is tryin' tae foist off a bludy woods colt on us. Th' bludy narve ... usin' poor dead Callum's name when he's nae heer tae defend himself." Malcolm said glowering at the boy, who locked eyes on him and uttered the name his uncle had counseled him to use. "I am Deke Fraser."

"Boolshit," said Malcolm. "Yer name is Fraser... loch ma name is Riel."

"For Christ sake." Ewan said, glaring at his father. "Do you always have to be such a god damned hardhead? This boy is the spitting image of Callum. Look at those eyebrows. Those eyes. He's a Fraser no doubt about it. His mother must be that girl Callum was seeing. The one from Riviere Qui Barre. I've heard rumors that she was carrying his child."

"Och," Malcolm growled. "He's nae a Fraser. Just a wee breed someone is tryin' tae foist off on us."

"Stop your racist nattering." Ewan's slapped an open hand against a plaster wall. "Stop that kind of crap right now. I don't doubt the boy. In fact, he is the picture of Callum when he was a little shaver."

Malcolm was gratified at the spark of emotion displayed by his son, who had returned from France an unemotional automaton. Malcolm had devised a strategy of goading Ewan with contrarian statements and racist remarks intended to raise his son's ire. Until now, this strategy had not yielded results but now -- with the appearance of a small boy who looked like a Fraser -- Malcolm succeeded in igniting his son's temper.

The Fraser family had suffered losses over the past years. Callum had entered the war in its final year and perished in France. Rona succumbed to the Spanish Flu in 1919 and Ewan, who spent time in the trenches before reconstructing railways in war-torn France and Belgium, had returned from the conflagration sound in body but not in mind. He had become a morose fellow who favoured the life of a recluse. He had returned to his job on the Grand Trunk Railway, now part of Canadian

National Railway system, where he was a 'hoghead', railway parlance for a locomotive engineer. When he wasn't on the road, he immersed himself in a book collection that covered three walls of his second floor bedroom.

Malcolm, who had also been a hog head, had retired to putter around his farm and grow potatoes, which he sold at the Market Square in Edmonton. His potato patch took up ten acres of his 160-acre farm and he leased out the remainder to wheat farmers. His bucolic lifestyle changed when two events combined to elevate the Frasers into the ranks of the middle class. In 1916 the province of Alberta voted to prohibit the sale and consumption of alcohol and Malcolm began using his potatoes as feedstock for a vodka-like potable, known as TLT (Turnip Lake Thunder). A local bootlegger and blind pig operator named Ozzie Callander bought all the TLT that Malcolm could produce.

Soon after, when he learned that the City of Edmonton was planning to expand northward, he engaged a surveyor to divide his land into residential lots. After annexation, the Fraser fortunes grew as a minor land boom occurred on his subdivided property. Malcolm retained the farm buildings and the acres on which they stood -- a holding that remained outside of the city -- facing across the boundary toward the recently established community of Calder.

The area was within walking distance of the CNR marshalling yard and railroaders, of many ethnic origins, bought or rented homes in the new community. In order to distinguish his home from neighbourhood residences, Malcolm hired a contractor to transform his one-storey brick farmhouse into a two-storey structure. Indoor plumbing, an electrical generating system, hot and cold running water, a modern kitchen and telephone service, were some of the improvements made to the Fraser residence.

"Holy Christ Dad." Ewan said brandishing one of Deke's rubber boots. "This boy's feet are bare in these boots. He's got frostbite on his toes. We need a bucket of hot water."

Malcolm nodded and left the room.

"I have socks," Deke said. "They came offa my feet. They're still in my boots"

"Christ, boy. We'll have to work like hell to save your toes." Ewan took a pail of water from Malcolm and placing it in front of the boy, plunged both of Deke's feet into the pail. The boy yelled in protest but did not cry as Ewan nodded to his father to help restrain the squirming child.

"We've got to keep his feet hot."

Both men worked on the boy's feet for several hours. Deke had stopped resisting and began to watch the massaging procedure with interest. When his toes became red and swollen, Ewan said, "The blood 's flowing into them. Now, we have to bandage 'em up."

With his feet dressed, Deke was conducted to a bedroom, which he would occupy for the next fifteen years.

The boy's feet healed and, over time, his quiet

strength and Scot-like stoicism won over Malcolm and Deke became a Fraser in name and deed. The boy's presence had a positive effect on Ewan, which pleased Malcolm even though he noticed that his son sometimes referred to the boy as 'Callum.'

When Malcolm discovered that Deke was a natural athlete, he began coaching the boy in the 'sweet science' of pugilism. Having been a light-heavy weight-boxing champion in the British Army, Malcolm had trained both of his sons as fighters. Deke, he felt, had the reflexes and dexterity that, with the proper training, could transform him into a champion.

The high water mark in Malcolm's life had occurred in 1913 when he traveled to Calgary and was in attendance at the Manchester Arena for a heavyweight encounter between American Luther McCarty and Canadian Arthur Pelkey; two so-called "White Hopes" touted as potential contenders to regain the heavyweight crown for the white race by defeating Jack Johnson, the black man who held the title. McCarty, the favourite, collapsed in the first round and died several hours later. Pelkey was held by the police for several days, but was released without charge. Malcolm dined out on the story until the end of his life.

As Deke became ring wise, Ewan decided to round out the boy's education by teaching him the rudiments of hockey. He built a facility that became a hub of wintertime activity in the Calder area. Two large areas of the farmyard were flooded in late autumn, one bordered with 40" high boards for hockey and one left open for recreational skating.

A born tinkerer and inventor, Ewan developed an ice machine, consisting of a 45-gallon drum laid horizontally upon a sled-like support. A tap on the low side of the drum released warm water into a perforated tray, which traversed the length of the barrel and distributed water onto strips of canvas that mopped the water on to the ice surface when pulled by skaters prior to games. A second 45-gallon drum was perched on a masonry platform, which housed a fire of coal briquettes that provided the heated water required to create a glassy ice surface.

An unused machine shed, heated by two Quebec heaters, provided changing facilities, stick racks and a grinder on the bench for skate sharpening. Hanging on a wall were skates of all sizes, as many of the children who showed up at the rink didn't own skates. The building also contained a ring and boxing accoutrements such as light and heavy bags.

A growing number of neighbourhood children began to show up on winter evenings and weekends. When larger boys bodied Deke and his contemporaries off of the ice, Ewan instituted a schedule, separating players into age groups for weekend tournaments. The tournaments became a popular venue for players, parents and the odd hockey scout. Malcolm was gratified to find his son involved in something other than his brooding, bookish existence and he developed a genuine affection for the small boy who had caused it to happen.

Ewan enjoyed success coaching Deke and his contemporaries. He instructed the boys in innovative methods that led to a succession of tournament wins. After a time he was requested to extend his expertise to older players and his innovative methods began to be emulated by other coaches. He devised methods -- some of them draconian -- like the device for keeping a player's head up when entering the offensive zone with the puck. He hung a necklace-like device featuring an upright needle around the player's neck. Players soon learned to keep their heads up when carrying the puck, although many of them had difficulty explaining the strange puncture wounds to their parents.

Another innovation was a wooden shield, known simply as the Board, a device that covered the goalmouth except for puck-sized holes in the upper and lower corners and in the lower middle area of the device. Deke fired pucks at the holes for hours to perfect his accuracy. Gifted with excellent hand-eye coordination, he soon learned that he could outplay and outshoot many older, more experienced boys.

In order to provide a settled environment for his nephew, Ewan had engaged a number of housekeepers over the past years, all of whom Malcolm had found to be lacking in one quality or another. It wasn't until Mingo Perala, a wartime comrade of Callum's, arrived with a young woman in tow that Malcolm's demanding requirements were met. Her name was Faith Talman and she became a permanent fixture in the Fraser household.

Convinced that, in Faith, he had found a proper mate for his son, Malcolm stipulated in his will that Ewan had to marry in order to inherit the estate. In 1930, Malcolm engineered a marriage between Ewan and Faith and then went to Scotland, where he remained until his death in 1935.

Chapter 3 - Tommy Flynn

London England – January 1917

THE MAN STOOD AT THE WINDOW smoking a Turkish cigarette. As he stared into the London overcast, his face was reflected in the leaded panes of glass in the tall windows and backlit by flames, which danced in the fireplace behind him.

"Aidan?"

He turned and smiled at the woman whose face was visible among the coverlets and quilts of a four-poster bed.

"Put out that noxious weed, and come back to bed you silly bugger! You're liable to freeze a very important part of your anatomy."

Chuckling, Aidan turned and pitched his cigarette into the fire. He untied his robe and shrugged it off of his shoulders, allowing the garment to slide to the floor as he strode quickly towards the bed and the welcoming space his companion provided by holding up a corner of the quilt.

"You were out like a light," he said as he moved toward her. "I thought I'd have a smoke."

"Oh, so the virile Canadian bull wore out the little Welsh heifer did he?"

Aidan stared at her for a moment before a surprised laugh popped his lips open and he exploded with laughter.

"Moira Evans, you are truly one of a kind. I can honestly say that I have never, in my entire life, met anyone like you."

"You mean that you've never met a wanton little trollop before? That's what my Aunt Gwyneth calls me."

"A wanton little trollop, eh? I like that." He gathered her in his arms. "Well then. Let's have some more wanton trollop behaviour."

Later, as they lay back and watched the light from the hearth play over the ceiling, Moira propped her head on an elbow and looked down at him.

"I just cannot understand why you are going back. You've done your bit. You have risked life and limb and, as a consequence, been grievously wounded for King and country. You know I could get you a staff appointment in a flash. My father has an in with Lloyd-George and could arrange it. You are, after all, a decorated war hero."

Aidan turned his face from her and was silent for some moments. Then, he turned back. "If I opt for a staff job and force myself to consort with those red-tabbed bastards. Will you marry me?"

"Oh, Aidan! Of course I will marry you. Oh my God, I can't believe my ears. I have been head over heels for you since we met. I just didn't think you felt the same way about me."

Aidan reached out and tweaked her cheek.

"You little Welsh ninny. Of course I love you."

Aidan's declaration led to a further bout of lovemaking that ended in mutual, satisfied slumber.

Awaking to sunlight streaming through the high cathedral style windows, Aidan opened his eyes to see Moira's smiling face. "Today," she declared. "I am going to speak to Pater about arranging an appointment for you. On Staff. Maybe in L.G.'s entourage."

"Anything but the Staff." Aidan said mournfully.

"Why do you hate the Staff so much?"

"One of my friends from university -- a fellow I enlisted with back when Gault formed the regiment -- gave in to political pressure and became a staff officer. He had served for many months at the front, from Frezenberg to the Somme. He was an excellent line officer and his men loved him and would have gone through walls for him. He came from an important political family back home and they wanted him back in one piece because they had plans for him. Big plans. Maybe Prime Minister someday."

"Ah." Moira said.

"None of the boys faulted him for taking a staff job. Hell, we were all glad that he was out of harm's way."

"And," Moira asked. "What is the point of all this?"

"The point is ... he couldn't stomach it."

"Stomach what?"

"Stomach being among the men who planned the deaths of so many good soldiers... almost every day... and did it from the safety of chateaus and castles in the rear! In disgust he transferred back to the unit and, before long bought a packet. All they found of him was one boot, complete with leg."

"Oh my god... that is terrible! When, if ever, do you think this ugly, stupid, inhuman masculine pissing match will end?"

"When Haig and Hindendorf run out of cannon fodder. You can bet that extremely sweet ass of yours that those craven bastards will never risk their own necks. But, m'dear." Aidan reached for her. "As Caesar said to Cleopatra, 'I am not prone to argue.'"

❈ ❈ ❈

Vimy France, April 1917

In the pre-dawn hours of April 9, 1917, large flakes of snow began falling on the men of the Canadian Corps. The first wave of attackers shivered with cold as they counted down to the moment when a creeping barrage would commence and lead them up the escarpment confronting them; a land mass almost 500 feet in height, honey-combed with German steel and concrete emplacements, dugouts and tunnels.

At 5:30 that morning every artillery piece available to the Canadian Corps -- almost 1,000 artillery pieces supplemented by over a hundred machine guns -- began pounding the ridge. Canadian gunners had timed a barrage that moved up the slopes of the ridge ahead of the attacking infantry, depriving the enemy of the customary lull between bombardment and attack. The men of the Canadian Corps advanced from their four-mile long start line in the valley of the Scarpe and moved up the heights of Vimy Ridge.

During the Somme campaign Aidan had seen barrages concentrate their fire on enemy wire and trench lines for hours before halting to allow the infantry to attack. The ensuing interval, between the cessation of the barrage and the infantry charge, gave the enemy adequate time to emerge from their deep, well-appointed underground emplacements and set up machine guns and field pieces with which to decimate the oncoming infantry. The attackers were cut down in windrows and left to rot in No Man's Land.

The Vimy action had been planned to leave nothing to chance. This time, the Germans would emerge from cover to stare into the business ends of Canadian rifles.

Aidan was attached to "C" Company of Princess Patricia's Canadian Light Infantry. After recovering from wounds inflicted during the Battle of Courcelette the previous year, and not as trained in Vimy procedures as his peers, he was detailed to act as a spotter for a team of snipers.

At 0430 he was summoned for a meeting at regimental HQ and he and CSM Bill Horton made their way in a growing storm into the chalk tunnels that housed the regimental headquarters.

They entered the tunnel complex and encountered hundreds of men filing out to take their positions on the line. The sounds of bombardment continued unabated as they made their way deeper into the network of passageways. Aidan, confused by the myriad tunnels and caverns, followed Horton who, without hesitation, led him to the Patricia's command post and the C.O. Colonel Adamson.

After a last minute briefing for line officers and NCOs, Aidan returned to his platoon and the men who awaited him in a chalk cavern.

"Well Cap," a sergeant asked. What do you think of this operation?"

"For openers," Aidan smiled. "We didn't have tunnels like this at the Somme."

"Surely this can't be worse than the Somme." Hat Hanson said.

"Nothin' could be worse than the fuckin' Somme." Bill Horton said. Even Fritzie put up signs saying 'Take it easy. We were at the Somme too."

The men, sobered by the mention of the Somme campaign, were silent for several moments. When Aidan had been wounded the previous year, and invalided to Britain for treatment, Moira

71

had wangled an appointment for him on Lloyd-George's staff. But, before his staff appointment was effective, his conscience had dictated that he return to the front, feeling that his men would require his experience and leadership. But now, as he stood among them -- men who were trained to the point where they could fulfill their duties blindfolded -- he realized that they didn't need him and he experienced a surge of regret at not having stayed in London with his beautiful young bride.

He stepped back and observed the men and felt proud to be in the company of such tough, capable soldiers. Through a number of battles and engagements, his countrymen had proven themselves to be the best-goddamned fighting men on the Western Front. When asked why Canadians were such effective soldiers, his old Sergeant Major Ian MacIsaac had explained it by stating, "Canada was created by the Scots so it was only natural that Canadian soldiers would inherit the Scottish warrior ethic and fight like Scots."

The Somme had taken its toll and he had seen a lot of new faces when he returned. Two of the old guard, CSM Bill Horton, the stalwart bald-headed farmer from the prairies, and Abel Talman, the laconic Alberta cowboy, whose amazing eyesight made him a sniper extraordinaire, were detailed to accompany Aidan during the action. Horton and Talman were to eliminate specific targets, such as enemy officers and NCOs, as identified by Aidan.

Abel checked the action on his Ross rifle, as

he had done several times during the past hour, prompting Horton to make a disparaging remark about the much-maligned weapon. The Ross was a rifle of Canadian design and manufacture, which excelled in controlled environments such as firing ranges and Bisley competition, but failed in the mud and gumbo of trench warfare. Its screw-type straight-pull bolt mechanism, which required frequent oiling, often failed to function when jammed with mud or irregular cartridges. The British Lee-Enfield had a lever type bolt, which would forcibly eject a spent round while jacking a new one into the chamber. At the battle of second Ypres, where the Germans launched their first major gas attack, Canadian troops were flanked on two sides by French colonial troops and left to hold a gap known as the Ypres Salient. After their allies broke ranks and fled, the Canadians -- informed by a quick-thinking medical officer to breathe through urine-soaked fabric to neutralize the chlorine gas -- stepped up to prevent the enemy from exploiting the gas attack. The Ross had failed miserably in the muddy conditions, leaving some frustrated men to use them as clubs.

"You're gonna wear that toy out with all that jackin' around." Horton said. "Now… if you carried one a' these." He hefted his Lee-Enfield, "You could use it as fer a crowbar and it would still shoot."

The cowboy shifted a chaw of tobacco from one cheek to another and grinned at Horton. "Yeah, and if I'd a thought to bring my old Sharps, I could've picked off old Kaiser Bill on the main street of Berlin and ended this war years ago."

"Aw, don't let this pot licker bullshit ya. He couldn't hit a bull in the ass with a scoop shovel ... even if someone held its head."

The men turned to look at a tall newcomer in their midst. Abel swiveled his head to confront the joker but his scowl transformed into a smile of recognition as he whooped and pumped the newcomer's hand. "Hey boys," he announced. "Meet Mingo Perala, the long drink of water I bin tellin' you about. We worked on the old Double B together."

Abel introduced his friend to Horton and Hanson, who welcomed Mingo into their midst. Horton said: "Hey Mingo, how come yer pal here," he hooked a thumb at Abel, "couldn't stick with you Donkey Wallopers?"

"Well," Mingo drawled. "When the Pats found out that Abel could shoot the pecker off a grasshopper at 500 yards, they snapped him up. I'm surprised there's any Huns left what with Abel and Jim Christie pickin' them off ever' day."

"Hey, Mingo," Hanson said, "You horse soldiers gonna ride up the ridge?"

"Nah. They dismounted us and fed us into the line as infantry reinforcements. I guess they think these new iron tanks are going to replace horses. Shit. Shetland ponies can run circles around them rust buckets."

"Well," Abel said, "Welcome to the PBI. You can sabre some Fritzies."

"Can't do that neither. They took away our cutlery. We're down to pig stickers," He tapped the sheathed sword bayonet attached to his belt.

Aidan returned to the gathering, after exchanging pleasantries with an acquaintance, and Abel pointed to Mingo. "Cap. This is my old compadre Mingo Perala. Mingo, this here's the best line officer on the Western Front, Captain Aidan Flynn."

"Pleased to meet you Mingo." Aidan said. "After the war I promised my wife Moira that we would visit the Rocky Mountains. Maybe we'll see you and Abel and that ranch he always brags about."

"You won't regret it Sir." Mingo said. "It's the sweetest place in this whole buggered-up world. When you come out, we'll take you and yer wife on a trail ride in the Rockies."

"Looking forward to it." Aidan smiled. "Keep your head down so we can keep that appointment in the mountains."

"You too Cap."

Aidan and his snipers left the chalk mine and proceeded out onto snow-covered ground on their way to an old trench line that would be their starting point. At the pre-arranged time, the men of the Third Division began their ascent of the ridge and Aidan and his companions began moving from location to location, picking off selected targets. Aidan had established a new vantage point when Talman tapped him on the shoulder.

"Heads up Cap. There's Boche behind us." Abel

mouthed the warning, his voice lost in the sounds of the bombardment.

Aidan's party had inadvertently set up a post several yards behind a German trench that had been filled with soil from a shell burst. As the Canadians were setting up their position, a number of German infantrymen had dug themselves out of the ruined emplacement and began firing at Aidan's party. He saw Talman and Horton rise to engage the enemy in hand-to-hand combat but when he moved to support them, he felt an impact akin to being hit on the chest with a baseball bat. He remembered traversing the moonscape of mine craters and shell holes amid the smoke and fire of the attack and recalled throwing a Mills bomb into a German dugout with his good arm and passing throngs of German prisoners being conducted down the ridge.

The sounds of battle around him faded to a swirling hum and he could no longer hear even the freight train-like sound of the artillery. Wispy memories of men shouting soundlessly, explosions and flashes of diffused light tantalized him until he saw only the swirling gray sky above him. He heard a ringing sound and was reminded of the musical sound of thousands of bayonet locking rings being engaged prior to the moment of attack. It was then that he realized that he was lying at the bottom of a shell hole, a hole partially filled with blood and human body parts. A German helmet beside him suddenly moved and he clawed his pistol from its holster. When the helmet rolled over, revealing the decapitated head of a young man being torn at by a large rat, Aidan lifted his pistol and blew the animal apart, adding to the carnage in the hole.

He lapsed in and out of consciousness for an indeterminate amount of time, aware of the men who rushed by him but unable to catch anyone's attention. Finally, in the bright light of day, he heard Abel Talman's voice. "Over here Bill. He's over here."

Aidan felt himself being lifted out of the crater, placed on a stretcher and carried back down into the valley.

"Captain Flynn ... you hear me?" Aidan's eyes fluttered and he became aware of Bill Horton's face above him. " You're at the aid station an' yer gonna be all right." Hat patted Aidan's good shoulder reassuringly before leaning down and speaking into his ear. "We took our objectives. La Folie Wood and the crest of the ridge are ours. We took the ridge."

Aidan attempted a smile but Horton had moved back to make room for someone else. Aidan opened his eyes again, this time to see the shocked countenance of his younger brother Liam. Liam who was supposed to be in medical school in Montreal.

For his part, Liam had heard that his brother had opted for a staff posting and would no longer be risking life and limb at the front. He was thinking that something was terribly wrong as his brother made a rattling gasp and lay still.

In a doctor's office on Harley Street in London,

Moira Evans-Flynn learned that she was with child.

After learning of Aidan's death, Moira retreated to her family home in Wales and, in December 1917 gave birth to a boy who she named Thomas Aidan Flynn. When the boy was six months old she sent him, in the care of her sister Bronwyn, to Aidan's family in Montreal.

Moira's father, a third-generation colliery magnate, was engaged in the war effort and rarely left London. Her mother had decided to sit out the war with a lover in Bermuda, leaving the Evans household in the care of Moira's youngest sister Glynis and a large staff of household retainers. Moira joined the army as an auxiliary nursing sister and, in June of 1918, was posted to the Basingstoke Hospital in Hampshire.

Chapter 4- Mingo

―――――――――――――――――――――――――――――

Fort MacLeod Alberta Summer 1916

WHEN THE WESTBOUND PASSENGER TRAIN PULLED into a sidetrack to allow the passage of a silk train, Mingo decided to get out and stretch his legs. Stepping down from the coach he found himself surrounded by some of the best looking horses he had ever seen. He ducked back onto the steps of the car but not quick enough to avoid spooking the animals. He winced as they scattered and made for open land adjacent to trackside loading pens.

"Git outta the way plowboy," a rider yelled at Mingo before spurring his mount vigorously and riding off in pursuit of the scattering horse herd.

Mingo watched as a group of cowboys contained the horses and streamed them into a holding corral. When all of the horses were inside, he ran over and closed the wide gate of the enclosure. The rider, who had yelled at him, rode up and began to crowd him between his horse and the corral. Not one to retreat, Mingo grasped the horse's bridle causing it to rear back on its haunches.

The rider's face twisted in anger and he lifted a braided rawhide quirt, looped around a wrist, and leaned forward to strike at Mingo. Before he could land a blow, another rider moved up and grabbed the whip. "Back off Hafner," the man said as he moved his own mount forward. Looking at Mingo he said. "You want to let go of the horse, kid?"

Mingo released the bridle and a ghost of a smile twitched his lips as he heard Hafner plead with the man twisting the quirt.

"Geez Talman, cut it out. Yer breakin' my wrist. Leggo!" The second rider was about to release him when Mingo raised a hand and pointed to the horse's bleeding flank.

"This the' way you fellers treat yer horses?"

"No it ain't." another rider, an older man in a graying goatee and range attire, interjected.

"Hafner. You step down from that hoss. Collect yer pay at the town office. Yer done on the Double B."

"What?" You lettin' some farmhand with pig shit on his shoes call the shots now?"

"You know who calls the shots. I've bin watchin' the way you treat saddle stock and defenseless animals. You and the Double B are done!"

Hafner dismounted and cast a withering glance at Mingo, who moved to return to the train. The older man rode up beside him.

"Where you bound amigo?"

"I'm goin' to Hillcrest Mines to get a job."

"Santa Maria. Why'd you want to do that? D'ya know that 200 men were kilt in that mine a couple of years ago? You'll git enough of that underground stuff after you croak. I saw the' way you handled yerself back there and I gather horses don't spook you so much."

"Bin around 'em all my life."

"I'm lookin' fer a good breaker. Interested?"

"I don't break horses," Mingo said. "I gentle 'em."

The man smiled, and said: "All the better, I'll take gentled horses over broken horses any day. Seventy a month and keep."

"Sounds good to me, Mingo reached up to shake the man's outstretched hand."

"What's yer handle?"

"Handle?"

"Yer name."

"My name is Mingo. Mingo Perala."

"What's that? Eyetalian?"

"Finn."

"Ah, a Finnlander, eh? Well Mingo, my name is Benitez. B.B. Benitez but you call me Ben; I run a horse outfit over on the Double B, a spread that runs from jest south of Pincher Creek to the border. We got a contract to supply saddle stock to the cavalry an' it looks like they're going' ta keep us busy as hell 'til the war ends. I just wish to hell they'd quit killin' all those good Alberta horses over there."

For the most part, Mingo fit in well with the personnel of the Double B. Part owner and ranch manager Bernardo Benito Benitez, who called himself a Texican, ran the show. The wiry little foreman had been a cowboy all of his working life, having worked trail drives from Texas to Montana, in the late eighties as a fourteen-year-old wrangler in charge of a remuda.

After a severe blizzard killed hundreds of cattle in southern Alberta in 1906, stockmen began replenishing their herds and Ben worked as a trail boss on a drive into Canada in 1907. He found the Alberta foothills, with their sheltered valleys, adequate water and grass, and warm Chinook winds, a perfect place to raise horses.

After the '07 trail drive, he met and married a local girl, leased a quarter section of land near Fort MacLeod and began supplying horses to the mounted police. The operation was never financially successful and his wife left him after three years of a hand-to-mouth existence.

Developing a time-consuming breeding program and waiting for his invoices to clear through the NWMP bureaucracy in Ottawa, finally did him in and he sold his stock, settled his debts and walked away from his ranch. He was lining up to buy a rail ticket to Calgary when a horseman rode up to the train platform.

"Don't buy that ticket, " the rider said as he sat, elbows folded on the saddle horn with four large, battle-scarred dogs lying in a loose semi-circle around his mount.

"What're you jawin' about, Abel?"

"Feller over at the hotel is lookin' fer ya."

"A process server no doubt." Ben said.

"No, it's some nob from the East. He's lookin' to start a horse ranch and he heard you were lookin' fer work."

"Well," Ben said. "He's a day late an' a dollar short then, cuz I'm through nursing broomtails. My wife left me and, after sellin' my herd and payin' her out, I ain't got a shinplaster to show fer all the years I bin cowboyin'. No tengo dinero. Time I got me a real job." After years among western Canadians, Ben's Spanish only manifested itself in the odd word or phrase.

"He says he's settin' up a big horse breeding operation in the foothills south a' Pincher Creek. Some Mountie muckety - muck told him that you raised some a' the best mounts they've ever had, so he wants to hire you. I told him that if you were on board, I would sign on too."

The men were surprised by a voice that emanated from the shadowed depot canopy: "I have heard that you are a dab hand with horseflesh Mr. Benitez." A man, looking not unlike Teddy Roosevelt, stepped out from the shadow and approached Ben with an extended hand. He was dressed in khaki from head-to-toe, jodhpurs, shirt and vest. His shiny brown riding boots and peaked Stetson were the only exceptions.

Ben reluctantly accepted the man's hand and turned to Abel, who had remained mounted. "I take it this is the feller you was goin' on about."

"Yep."

"I sir," the man said, shaking Ben's hand vigorously, "am Senator Thomas Buxton of

Montreal. I learned to play polo when I served as a cavalryman in the South African War and it is my belief that superior polo ponies can be bred in the foothills of Alberta. These ponies could also be exported to the British Isles and other polo playing nations. And, I might add, fulfill a need here at home among a growing population of 'remittance men.' I might also add that I am the party who purchased your breeding stock."

"Well, that's nice. I hope you can teach 'em to chase a ball."

"But, Mr. Benitez. In addition to your horses, I would also like you and your expertise involved in this enterprise."

"Sorry to disappoint you compadre, but, I got to get me a job with some kind of future. Cowboyin' jest don't cut it anymore. I'll never get my wife back if I sign on with a brush-popping outfit so I'm off to Calgary. I got a lead on a job makin' horse collars."

"My dear fellow." The man said. "I'm not hiring you."

"Then, why in hell," Ben was becoming irritated, "are you wastin' my time?"

"I am looking for a partner. Not an employee. When I embarked upon this venture, I hired people to find someone who could run it in my absence. From all of the reports I have received. You are that man. I will not have the opportunity to visit this area often, due to my other duties, so I need someone I can trust to run the operation."

Ben held up a hand: "I ain't got money to throw into no partnership."

"But sir. You will earn a fifty per cent share by running the operation. You will also draw a regular salary."

"Well then," Ben said, stepping out of line, "it appears that you've just made yerself a deal."

The ranch, which was born that day, was called the Double B. and the brand featured two interlinked B's facing one another.

The remittance men, that the Senator alluded to, were usually the second or third sons of titled or wealthy merchant families in Britain. For various reasons -- most notably bad behaviour -- they were sent off to the colonies and financed with a monthly 'remittance' from home to keep them in a remote location where they could no longer embarrass their families. Many of them were excellent horsemen and polo players, but they didn't seem to be good at anything else.

Used to having servants 'do' for them, and supremely confident that they could accomplish anything they set their minds to, they became objects of derision in a frontier society that didn't suffer fools. Yet, when war was declared almost all of them enlisted. That action prompted Bob Edwards of 'The Calgary Eye Opener' to write: 'they were green but they weren't yellow.'

The Double B became a mecca for polo players, a number of whom were Remittance Men. One of them, Jonathan Benwood, the second son of an Earl, showed up to inspect some polo ponies and ended up staying on as a horse trainer and polo instructor. At the outbreak of war in 1914, Benwood enlisted in a cavalry regiment but to his chagrin, found himself stationed in southern Alberta as a horse buyer for the army. Because of the quality horseflesh produced on the ranch, he spent most of his time on the Double B.

Abel Talman became a good friend to Mingo. His job was to hunt down predators that threatened the mares and foals. With the help of his bear dogs, Abel dramatically reduced the number of predators in the area and the ranch's outbuildings usually had the hide of some large carnivore stretched on them as Abel, who was also an accomplished leather worker, kept the ranch hands in vests, coats and chaps of grizzly, cougar and wolf skin.

The Talman family had emigrated from Utah in 1890, the year that polygamy was banned by the Mormon Church in the United States. Abel's father Nephi and his family -- consisting of his two wives, six children and younger brother Moroni -- crossed the border with three other plural families. They established a communal cattle ranch on the Milk River where Moroni, who fancied himself a prophet, made a vow to make Alberta the new Deseret.

Abel was expelled from the commune at an early age after making the mistake of wooing a young girl of his own age, a girl who, unbeknownst to him, had been selected for his uncle Moroni. At age fourteen, Abel was summarily ejected from the commune.

After doing menial jobs in and around Pincher Creek, he moved further west and found work as a wolfer, perfecting his marksmanship and working in that business until he earned enough cash to purchase an 1874 model Sharps .40 calibre rifle, a saddle horse, a packmule and some bear dogs. He offered his services to the local ranchers and sheepherders and spent a year with a sheep operation near Longview, before hiring on with Ben Benitez's horse operation in 1912. Another good friend was Willie Shingoose, a horseman and rodeo competitor from a rodeo family of the Peigan Nation. Willie had helped snub up 'Cyclone,' a famous bucking horse who had never been ridden, for his friend Tom Three Persons at the 1912 Calgary Stampede. Three Persons went on to ride the horse into submission earning a world championship.

Mingo didn't hit it off with all of the ranch hands, the exception being the bull cook, Erwin Hafner. Erwin's duties consisted of washing dishes, helping out around the cookhouse and keeping the bunkhouse in order... tasks that didn't require too much brainpower. He enjoyed working with Abel but he gave Mingo short shrift as he held him responsible for getting Freddie fired.

Erwin's life would have been simpler if had it not been for Freddie, who, although barred from the Double B, often snuck around to borrow money and have Erwin raid the larder for him.

Erwin hadn't always been a simple custodian. In his youth he had been the toast of northern

Montana. His father, Gerhard Hafner emigrated from Austria in 1875 and found work on a cattle ranch in the Bitterroot Valley. In short order, he married the ranch owner's daughter and assumed management of the spread when his new father-in-law handed him the reins. The ranch, known as the Turkey Track, prospered under Gerhardt's management; in addition to increasing the cattle herd, he procured a contract to provide mounts for the United States Cavalry.

His sons, Erwin, born in 1880, and Freiderich, born in 1885, grew up working on the ranch. Erwin was a natural born cowboy. He rode horses from the age of two, and loved every minute of ranch life. As a young man, he was well liked by members of the ranching community and almost every mother of a marriageable female, campaigned for his attention. Long before Roy Rogers was given the title 'King of the Cowboys' Erwin was known by that sobriquet in the Bitterroot Valley.

Freddie was another breed of cat. Possibly, because his brother was so popular, Freddie decided to go in another direction. At sixteen, he organized a gang of fellow malcontents and began rustling cattle. They'd take three or four head a night and trail them to a confederate at a stockyard, who would assimilate them with animals being shipped to Chicago. It was a 'cash on the barrel-head, no questions asked' arrangement and it financed the boys on binges in some of the smaller communities in the valley.

As it happens with most first time criminals,

the boys were soon apprehended. Tracked by a stock detective they were brought before the courts where Freddie blamed it all on his accomplices, several of whom were in their twenties. Because of his grandfather's political connections, he was placed under the supervision of his older brother who promised to teach him right from wrong. Erwin promised to give his younger brother a Bible and have him memorize and recite a scripture for the family each evening at the dinner table.

Freddie requested a grace period before first his recitation and was cheered up by the events that transpired at a rodeo in Missoula soon afterward. Erwin had drawn a large Canadian-bred bucking horse and, after two bone-jarring crow hops, was unseated. As he fell over the horse's hindquarters, the animal's right leg shot out and caught Erwin with a hoof to the back of his head.

From that moment on, life on the ranch changed. The shining star of the family and the heir to the Turkey Track was no longer the charismatic cowboy that everyone knew and loved. After months of hospitalization, Erwin emerged as a hollow-eyed, shambling, shadow of his former self who fixed upon his brother and followed him around like a faithful dog.

At first Freddie reveled in the role-reversal but soon found it to be problematic. Every time he turned around, Erwin was there, in the same shirt and overalls that he always wore, looking anxiously to his brother for direction. Freddie resented his brother's presence and was about to light out on his own when his father approached him with a proposition.

Hannah Hafner had been so depressed by her elder son's condition that she took to her bed and refused to leave it. Gerhard, who had become ashamed of his brain-damaged son, asked Freddie to take Erwin to a ranch run by an acquaintance in Canada. Gerhard promised to provide Freddie with the necessities of establishing a ranch of his own across the line. As a bonus, Gerhard gave Freddie an upfront $500 in cash, to take his brother north.

The following week, Freddie and Erwin rode through the gate under the Turkey Track sign for the last time mounted on two of Gerhard's best saddle horses and trailing a Hereford bull and two heifers. Tied to Erwin's saddle was a packhorse laden with provisions and new gear.

After stopping at every saloon and whorehouse between Missoula and the border, the brothers crossed the line riding bareback on two mules. Over the course of their trip, Freddie had drunk or gambled away the $500.00 bonus, plus the saddle stock and packhorse. The bull and heifers were stolen when he left them in a gully near a saloon.

Gerhard had given Freddie a letter of introduction to Ben Benitez at the Double B and the missive, which mentioned breeding stock, gear and good saddle horses, puzzled Ben. When he questioned Freddie, who hadn't bothered opening the letter, he was told that they had been high jacked on the trail. When Ben offered to write Gerhard, Freddie became vocal about 'showing the old man' that he could start a ranch without help from his father. Ben, while leery of the brothers but shorthanded by the war, hired them.

Freddie proved to be lazy and incompetent with a mean streak a mile wide and he finally exhausted Ben's patience during the incident at the tracks. Erwin had been prepared to quit his job and follow his brother but Ben persuaded him to stay because he did his job well and because Freddie hadn't been seen in town since he drank up his back pay. Word had it that he had returned to Montana.

Before long, Freddie surfaced at the ranch. Under cover of darkness, he entered Erwin's sleeping quarters and persuaded his brother to provide him with food and any liquor he could lay his hands on. Erwin collected food for his brother but refused to provide him with liquor.

Freddie holed up in an unused line shack where Erwin would bring him food every week. On one occasion Freddie talked his brother into inviting Sunny Duchene, the ranch cook's daughter, and a girl Abel was courting, on a berry-picking expedition. Erwin said he would make them coffee when they arrived but, when Sunny entered the cabin she encountered Freddie, dressed in long johns and a hat. She turned to escape but found Erwin blocking the doorway.

"Now, you jest relax Sunny." Freddie grinned wolfishly while undoing the lower buttons on his underwear. "This ain't goin' to hurt a bit. You can jest close yer eyes and pertend that Abel is on top a' ye. From now on I'm gonna be doin' this regular."

Without hesitation, Sunny picked up a frying pan from the top of the stove and clocked Freddie on the side of the head. "Ye goldam bitch," he screamed, staggering back. "Now yer in for it." Turning to his brother, he yelled.

"Grab her and th'ow her on the bunk."

Erwin stood unmoving in the doorway prompting his brother to demand. "Ye dumb doorknob! I said th'ow her on the bunk and rip her pants off." Erwin remained frozen but, without warning, flew headlong into the room checking his forward motion by grabbing Freddie. Mingo appeared in the doorway with his Winchester saddle gun held across his chest. Nodding to the girl, he said: "Get behind me Sunny."

As Sunny walked around Erwin toward the doorway, Freddie leapt out of the open window. Mingo walked over to the window, levered a round into his rifle and fired.

'Ja kill 'im?" Erwin said, an anxious look on his face.

"Nah! Just shot his hat off."

Mingo turned to Sunny. "You head back to the ranch. I'll take Erwin and Freddie into Pincher and hand 'em over to the law."

"Don't do that Mingo. Please. I'm not supposed to be out here. Ma will give me what for if she finds out. She'll tell Abel for sure."

"Well then, just what th' hell were you doin' out here with these monkeys?"

Sunny pointed to Erwin. "He's my friend. I don't want him to go to jail. It's always Freddie's fault when Erwin gets in trouble. We were picking berries when we went into the line shack to make some coffee. Freddie was there."

Mingo reluctantly allowed Erwin to leave with Sunny. He realized that the man was brain-damaged with no history of violence.

"Get him outta here. I'm gonna collect Freddie."

Mingo found Freddie cowering under an outcrop. The man was hysterical, "Oh, please Mingo. Don't kill me. I promise I'll leave the country." Tears streamed down his cheeks as he raised his hands and stood in front of Mingo's mount. Mingo looked down from his saddle and bit down on his bottom lip to keep from laughing at the ridiculous figure Freddie presented. Hatless and bootless and garbed only in his long johns, Freddie pleaded for his life as he teetered on the edge of a ravine.

After delivering Freddie to the police, Mingo returned to the ranch to find that he was to take part in a rush delivery of horses to the army at Camp Sarcee near Calgary.

Soon after Canada had entered the war on Germany, Senator Buxton had descended upon the ranch with orders for hundreds of horses for the Canadian Expeditionary Force. He implored his ranch hands to stay at home, stating that they could do more for the war effort by training saddle stock than they could by going overseas. Some of the hands didn't have an opinion on the war and stayed put. Others, like Jon Benwood, had enlisted as soon as war was declared.

Willie, Abel and Mingo delivered a number

of trained saddle horses, which were allocated to infantry officers who had never ridden horseback. The Double B cowboys were asked to stay on and instruct the officers in horsemanship. They did such a good job that they were hired by the military as civilian contractors. Then, in a weak moment, in a Calgary saloon, the trio decided to sign up with the Lord Strathcona's Horse regiment.

❋   ❋   ❋

Near Amiens France March 1918

A procession of horsemen, their steel helmets and rubber capes shining with rain, picked their way through the ruins of a French village. Each rider led an unsaddled horse tethered closely to his own mount.

A motorcyclist rode in advance of the cavalrymen; leading them through and around the debris of devastated buildings. He followed a supply route that had been cleared to allow teamsters to come up at night with provisions and ordnance. When he reached the outskirts, he brought his machine to a stop and waited for the horsemen.

"Well, Sarge," he addressed the lead rider. The Strathconas are bivouacked down there in the trees. A sentry half way down the trail will challenge you. He'll direct you to your unit."

"Thanks partner," Mingo Perala touched the brim of his helmet in a two-fingered salute and, turning in his saddle, wordlessly signaled his men of the change in direction. As the horsemen turned and descended into the Avre river valley, the motorcyclist continued on, leading a procession of mule-drawn wagons to the front.

For hours the cavalrymen had ridden through a landscape ruined by continuous German shelling. The enemy had been strengthened by the addition of 50 divisions from the Russian Front -- following the collapse of Tsarist Russia -- and was making a concerted effort to split the British and French armies at the railhead centre of Amiens. If the Germans were successful, the French would have to retreat south to defend Paris and the British would have to fall back to protect their supply lines at the Channel ports. The Germans would move up the middle and seize the railhead, a move that would allow them to ship their large siege guns within range of Paris.

During the previous month, the Germans had advanced within 60 kilometres of Amiens and were close to taking the town of Moreuil, which was situated on a wooded ridge overlooking the approaches to the railhead. Brig.-Gen Jack Seeley, who commanded the Canadian Cavalry Brigade, realized that whoever held the ridge would hold Amiens and whoever held Amiens would win the war.

Earlier in the conflict, as trench warfare had not lent itself to cavalry operations, Canadian horse soldiers had been dismounted and relocated to the trenches as infantrymen. But, shortly after the German breakthrough in 1918, regiments such as the Lord Strathcona's Horse, Fort Garry Horse and the Royal Canadian Dragoons, were remounted to provide reconnaissance and a mobile strike force.

Although he had been told to wait for further orders, Seely had received intelligence that the enemy had taken Moreuil and was advancing on Amiens. With the French retreating on his right and the British in a confused state, he was considering his options as Mingo and his replacements were entering the river valley.

The rain began to abate as Mingo guided his big Waler stallion, Spud, onto a descending trail into a wooded valley where the trees had all been 'topped' by artillery barrages. As the cyclist had predicted, halfway down the trail, a rain-caped figure rode out of the trees and demanded: "Halt. Who goes there?"

"Farrier Sergeant Perala with replacements and remounts."

"F'Chrissake Mingo," the sentry said. "What th' hell you doin' back here? Thought you had a cushy job back in Blighty."

"Aw, I was worried that you pot lickers weren't treating my horses right. Decided to come take a look for myself. I hear that this war's almost over anyways."

"Oh yeah? Tell that to Kaiser Bill. I hear that one-armed popinjay is planning to come bustin' through here. Makin' a run fer the Channel I hear. Anyway, I'll be in shit if I don't keep you guys movin'. Who you reporting to?"

"Lieutenant Benwood."

"By the smell of it, Benwood's boys are boiling'

up their boots about a half-mile down the track. You'll smell 'em before you see 'em."

As his column progressed further down the trail, Mingo smelled the familiar odour of bully beef being fried and he sensed the presence of many horses. Soon afterward he led his men into a clearing in the truncated forest.

A number of khaki-clad men were preparing meals for themselves and their horses. Mingo turned to the men behind him. "Find yourselves some cover boys and get them remounts over to the Regimental Sergeant-Major over at the horse lines."

"Hey Sarge."

Mingo turned to see one of his replacements, a boy named Callum Fraser, extending a package to him.

"What's all this?" Mingo said.

"It's just some stuff for my dad." The boy said. "The fellows tell me you've bin through a lot of battles and never bin scratched."

"Jesus kid!" Don't jinx me."

"Oh. Sorry Sarge. What I mean is...would you see that my dad in Edmonton gets this. If... I don't make it?"

"Stop that shit." Mingo said dropping the package into a saddlebag. "I'll hang on to it until you can take it back. Now get over to the RSM."

"Thanks Sarge. I appreciate it. I wrote your name and my dad's name on it." The boy nudged his horse into motion and headed for the horse lines.

Mingo felt a tap on his left leg and looked down to see the smiling face of Lieutenant Jon Benwood.

"Well, if it isn't my favourite brush popper. I see you brought me a new mount."

"Yep...I hand delivered this hammerhead all the way from Blighty just so you can ride him into a hornet's nest of Huns like you did at Guyencourt last year."

"Good old Bongo." The officer said, a wistful tone in his voice. "That old hay-burner loved to lay into the Boche. "

"Yeah," Mingo said. "Old Bongo took out his share a' them that day but he couldn't take out that trench mortar."

"No. He couldn't beat that mortar round." Benwood was silent for a moment then his eyes came to rest on Mingo's mount. He ran a hand over the horse's neck.

"Good looking horse. What's his name?"

"Spud."

"Spud. How did you come up with a tag like that?"

"Well...he loves potato peels and, if the mess hall boys have 'em, apple peels. Anyway. You can't have Spud. But you can have this fella over here." Mingo nodded to the horse on Spud's right side. He untied the lead rope that attached to the horse and handed it to Benwood. "Here he is. Trained him myself."

Benwood accepted the halter rope and spent some time inspecting the animal. Turning to

Mingo, he said: "Well...he is one tough looking son-of-a-bitch, Mingo. He reminds me of how Kipling described a warhorse. 'The mouth of a bell and the heart of Hell and the head of the gallows tree.'"

"Yeah," Mingo said, he's not the prettiest pony in the paddock but he'll run over anyone you point him at."

"Well, if he has your seal of approval that's good enough for me."

"What you goin' to call 'im."

"I'm not naming them anymore. I've had too many shot out from under me. Now, I try not to get too attached to them."

"He'll be your best friend out there." Mingo nodded toward the front where the sounds of bombardment were growing louder.

"I know. I know. Tell you what." Benwood launched himself onto the back of the unsaddled horse. "If he and I make it through this funnel of airborne shit, I'll name him. You fixing to get out of here before that particular airborne material hits the fan?"

I'm supposed to head back to Blighty with some casualties tomorrow. I signed up as a horse soldier but the bastards put me in the mud and shit of the trenches. I would like to go on a horse patrol before I go."

"Christ Mingo. You're too good a horse mechanic to get yourself killed in some stupid pileup. Go back to Blighty and do what you do best."

"I'm not kiddin' Jonny. What squadron is my best bet?"

Benwood shook his head and looked at Mingo. "You bloody hardhead. Try "C" Squadron. Flowerdew's going out in an hour or so. I'm sure he'll take on a seasoned hand. Got your sabre honed?"

"Shaved with it this morning." Mingo said.

Benwood guffawed and touched his heels to the horse's flanks.

"Good luck you crazy Finn bastard." He shouted as his mount carried him away.

Flowerdew was of the same opinion as Benwood. Mingo was a valuable asset as a farrier, horse medicater and trainer. But, he also knew him to be a seasoned combat veteran and so he accepted him into "C" Squadron on a temporary basis.

"You make damn sure you survive Perala, because if I lose you out there, my name will be mud. Be ready to mount up at first light."

"Yes sir. You won't regret this sir." Mingo straightened and gave an elaborate salute.

"Get outta here." Flowerdew said.

After leaving Flowerdew, Mingo joined a group of men grooming their mounts at the picket line; a long rope to which numerous horses were tied. He renewed acquaintances with a Pincher Creek Mountie named Fenn Halliday as well as Jack Willoughby, another Mountie, Tom Mackie and bugler Reg Longley. To a man they expressed surprise at his desire to ride with the squadron. As he groomed Spud and fed him some oats and potato peels, he argued that he had been unhorsed back in '17 and ended up in the trenches. Before the war ended he wanted to see some action from the back of a horse.

As "C" Squadron passed Brigade Headquarters, General Seely rode out and accompanied Flowerdew, advising him of the task assigned to the squadron. The enemy was being pushed to the east, out of Moreuil Wood, by Canadian Cavalry units and "C" Squadron's task was to engage the Germans as they exited the woods. They were to hold them until Lieutenant Harvey, who had dismounted his squadron and entered the wood, came up to reinforce them. A total of six Canadian cavalry squadrons were to be engaged.

Mingo found himself riding knee-to-knee with Willie Shingoose, who grinned at the prospect of the impending action. He opened several buttons on his tunic and pulled out a long war club. The weapon was made of a crotched tree branch holding a large egg-shaped stone fixed by rawhide thongs. Willie hung a loop-affixed to the handle of the primitive hammer around his left wrist and shook the club menacingly.

"What the hell is that?" Mingo said.

"Old family heirloom." Willie grinned.

"Christ, how much does that thing weigh?" Mingo said.

"Nine pounds," the young Peigan grinned. I'm, gonna drum out a tune on some Fritzie noggins today."

As the horsemen turned a corner and emerged from the forest, they became aware of two lines of German infantry emerging from the woods and advancing in the direction of Amiens. When the Germans became aware of the Canadian horsemen, there was a moment of hesitation before they mobilized and began to deploy their weapons.

Flowerdew lifted his sabre, turned in his saddle and shouted: "It's a charge boys. It's a charge!" With a roar "C" Squadron spread into attack formation and made for the enemy.

Reg Longley was fatally wounded as he lifted his bugle for the charge but by then, the charge was well under way with horsemen leaping over the fallen bugler and making for the German lines. Mingo tucked his head behind Spud's neck and pointed his sabre in the direction of the enemy. He made a silent prayer that he would not leave his weapon stuck in a German as he had done with so many straw dummies on the practice field. Willie rode beside him whooping, waving his war club in one hand, his sabre in the other. The thundering sound of hoof beats shook the ground as the Canadian horsemen galloped over the undulating terrain that led up to their objective. Shellfire flew over their heads when they were in the depressions and blew some of them out of their saddles as they emerged onto high ground. Behind the charging cavalry the ground was strewn with dead and dying men and horses.

Mingo and Spud reached the German advance lines -- the charge had taken just over a minute -- and Mingo found himself in a sea of bucket-shaped helmets. He leaned from his saddle and began slashing and thrusting at the men on the ground. He wasn't certain if he was doing any damage until he noticed that his blade was running red with blood. Spud surged through the German infantrymen like a bowling ball and Mingo suddenly realized that the big stud had carried him through both German lines.

Wheeling, man and horse charged the enemy from their rear, cutting a swath through the defenders. Then Mingo leaned from his saddle and lost his sword in the torso of a German solder. "Shi-it!" He yelled as he pulled his revolver and emptied it at the enemy. Dropping the empty pistol, he pulled his carbine from its scabbard. He was about to jack a round into the breech, when Spud collapsed under him. Mingo was thrown from his saddle and, before he hit the ground, his last thoughts were for his horse.

"Hey, he's awake."

Mingo recognized the voice of Jon Benwood, who was hobbling toward him with the help of a walking stick. He opened his eyes and said, "Where the hell am I?"

"Why, you are in the Basingstoke hospital, old sock. Looks like the war is over for you...and me." Benwood said, pointing to an empty pants leg.

"What happened to me?" Mingo made an effort to lift his head but excruciating pain behind his eyes caused him to fall back on the pillow.

"Take it easy old boy." Benwood said. "You've had a bad go of it. As Ben Benitez would say, 'You look like you were et by a bear and shat out over a cliff.' You took a couple of rounds in the legs and you landed on your head. The sawbones says you have a severe concussion. You've been out for weeks."

"What happened to Spud?"

"I'm sorry old chap. A machine gun took him out. He didn't make it."

"Did he suffer?"

"Willie saw to him. According to Willie that horse of yours seemed more pissed off than wounded. He was one great horse. Cavalrymen are going to talk about you and Spud for years. You remember what I said about that horse you brought me?"

Mingo nodded and winced in pain. "Yeah. How did he do?"

"He acquitted himself admirably, so admirably that I have decided to name him Spud. If that's O.K. with you."

Mingo kept his head immobile but gave Benwood a thumb up.

"I'm glad you made it. How did it all turn out?"

Benwood propped his cane against the wall and dropped into a chair. He was silent for a moment, then he said: "From a military standpoint, it was a success because we stopped the Hun from taking Amiens. Most of the boys didn't survive though. Flowerdew got a V.C. ... posthumously. You're getting a gong... a Military Medal."

"What about that kid, the one who came out with me. Fraser? How did he make out?"

Benwood shook his head. "Sorry old boy ... he didn't make it."

"God dammit." Mingo slammed his fist on the bed and winced in pain.

"Hold on old fellow. I'll find your nurse."

The next time Mingo opened his eyes he beheld the face of a beautiful young woman and assumed he was looking at an angel. She moved away and he heard the voice of Willie Shingoose. "You're awake!"

"I musta dozed off." Mingo said.

"Dozed off? Christ! You bin out for weeks. They said you were in a coma and maybe never comin' out."

"That's bullshit." Mingo said as he attempted to prop himself on his elbows.

"Easy, easy." Willie grabbed his friend's shoulders and lowered him back to his pillow.

"I was just talkin' to Benwood. He was goin' for a nurse."

"Jesus, Mingo. Benwood bought it at Moreuil."

"That can't be. I was just talkin' to him." Mingo's eyes moved around the room "Where th' hell am I anyway?"

"You're in the Basingstoke Hospital."

"Is the war over?"

"Nope, but, it's almost done. Our boys and some ANZACs broke through the German lines and put old Fritzie on the run."

"Benwood told me you looked after Spud.

"He took a m.g. burst in the chest and was gone soon after I got to him. I dragged you off into the wood and left you behind a tree. At the time, I didn't know if you were dead or alive."

"Thanks partner. I just don't understand how I could've bin talkin' to Benwood if he was dead."

"Aah. He was just a ghost who decided to drop in on you." Willie said, "I seen lot's of ghosts this past while. But, here comes the sawbones, I better bugger off." He stood and Mingo grabbed his sleeve.

"What about the horses? They shipping the horses back home?"

"No. The cold-hearted bastards in Ottawa have actually sold some to slaughterhouses. They say it's too expensive to ship 'em back to Canada so, some a' those beautiful horses will be pullin' plows and some are goin' to be used for meat."

"Jesus," Mingo whispered. "Then I'm glad old Spud went out the way he did. Of course, he'd have kicked the shit out of any farmer that tried to hitch him to a plow."

When Mingo had awakened and beheld what he assumed to be an angel, the angel had a similar reaction. In her memoirs, 'the angel' Moira Evans-Flynn wrote that the big man with the wise gray eyes had 'looked into her very soul.'

After the end of hostilities, Moira began to use her portion of her family's resources to campaign against future wars and champion the rights of women. It was her contention the empowerment of women would put an end to wars. No women would blithely surrender the sons they bore to warmongers and war makers even though men had sacrificed themselves and their sons on the altar of empire and moneyed corporations for centuries.

The press lost no time in labeling her 'Moira the Red', and she became known as a rabble-rouser on several continents. In addition to her work for women's suffrage, she also became an advocate for organized labour. She donated and raised funds for Republican Spain against Franco and his fascist cohorts and became an ardent supporter of Dr. Norman Bethune and his work in Spain and China. When she was in North America, she and Mingo would spend time together. When she was away they lived separate lives.

Chapter 5 – Faith

Southern Alberta -1916

PRIOR TO HIS ENLISTMENT IN THE army, Abel received a hand-written note, delivered by a horse trader, in which his sister Faith asked for his help in delivering her from the commune where she had been selected to become the third wife of a fifty-year old man. She was twelve years old.

Abel and Mingo and Royal Northwest Mounted Police Constable Fenn Halliday, rescued the girl from the religious compound without incident. Her father was in Utah leaving his brother Moroni as the de facto leader of the commune and, as the rescuers rode out in a phalanx around Faith on her pinto, Moroni emerged from a building and loudly accused Abel of going against God's law. He called it a transgression that would not go unpunished. The threat occasioned Constable Halliday to turn his horse and ride back to the self-appointed Prophet.

"The only law that's been broken around here," he said. "is Canadian law. If I were you I would not be uttering threats. That is a breach of the law that will not go unpunished."

Word came soon after, that an altercation had taken place between Abel's father Nephi and Moroni, causing the Prophet, and a group of followers, to depart the Milk River commune and establish a settlement across the U.S. border on a promontory known as Bug Mountain.

Abel made arrangements to lodge his sister with the family of a retired Mountie in Calgary, where she began her formal education, and went on to make the fateful trip to Sarcee Camp and enlistment in the cavalry.

After the war, the men returned to the Double B to find that many changes had taken place on the ranch. Senator Buxton had succumbed to a heart attack in 1917 and his family in Montreal had moved in to liquidate the Alberta operation. They sent an agent to dispose of the remaining horse herd, clean out the bank account, sell the property and dismiss Ben Benitez.

When the agent reported that the foreman had documents to prove that he was half-owner of the ranch, they decided that they would go to court to have their father ruled incompetent at the time the contract was signed. This angered Ben, who engaged Paddy Nolan, a Calgary lawyer, who negotiated with the family on his behalf. Working through the courts to freeze the ranch's bank accounts, and placing liens on its buildings and stock, Nolan elicited a settlement that made Ben a wealthy man. He never did win his wife back and, after hearing that the horses he had raised and sent overseas, were being slaughtered in abattoirs in Europe, he left the country in disgust and returned to Texas.

After a nostalgic look around their old stamping grounds the trio found their way to a 'blind pig' outside of Pincher Creek. Bootleg joints, operating outside of the law, were among the few places to get a drink as Prohibition had taken hold in Alberta in 1916. The men gathered around a table and began to ponder their future. No ranchers were hiring and the ones that were, were disreputable outfits that made a habit of cheating their hands.

Willie spoke of a bootlegger, who was stocking up saloons in Montana with Canadian whisky and homebrew.

"Why they buyin' bootleg hooch?" Mingo said.

"Haven't ya heard?" Abel interjected. "The Yanks are goin' dry on the first a' the year."

"Whatya mean 'dry,'" Mingo said.

"Booze." Willie said. "No more booze. Bootleggers are gonna be kings. They made it the law that all liquor, in the U.S of A. is goin' to be illegal as of January 1, 1920.

"Well," Mingo drained his glass and rose from the table. "Let's go find out how this bootlegging business works."

After some research, they made a connection with a Calgary distiller who was ostensibly pro-ducing 'medicinal' liquor for distribution through drug stores, but also seeking opportunities to ship product to a larger market in the States. The boys firmed up a deal with the distiller and another one with a Lethbridge brewer and then made contact with an American agent, who paid top dollar for their merchandise.

The boys hired Barley Thornton and Vincent 'Pardee' Paradis -- two muleskinners who had seen action in France – to convey the goods across the border. Both men owned a team of the hardworking animals who carried the liquid cargo that Mingo, Abel and Willie delivered to Montana.

After six months of pocketing good money and anxious to pursue other interests, Willie withdrew from the venture to spend more time on the rodeo circuit. Abel and Mingo didn't want to continue without him and decided to end their smuggling career with one last run.

Abel was riding drag, at the rear of the pack train, when the sound of gunfire froze him in the saddle. He nudged his bay mare into a gallop and overtook the whiskey-laden mules as echoes of the shots sounded through the wooded valley. He rode to the head of the column bringing it to a halt.

Mingo had been riding point, several hundred yards ahead of the pack train, when the gunfire erupted. Reacting instinctively to the bark of a large calibre rifle, he withdrew his saddle gun and, with the echo of the gunshots ringing in the canyon, he turned his buckskin stallion around, slapped the big horse on the rump and sent it galloping back down the trail toward the pack mules.

He found cover among a stand of wolf willows and levered a round into his carbine. He squeezed off a shot into the treetops to signal his position to Abel and to freeze the shooter or shooters in their present positions. He levered a second round into the rifle and fired again before darting across the trail and burrowing into the underbrush.

Abel rode up to Pardee, who stood holding the bridle of Mingo's stud and examining it for injury.

"What's the story?" Abel asked as he dismounted and handed the reins of his bay to Barley, who had also dismounted and was nervously brandishing a .38 calibre Smith and Wesson revolver.

"Put up that popgun up kid." Abel said. "You're liable to shoot a hole in some a' our goods."

Abel pulled a canvas wrapped object from the scabbard behind his saddle, placed it on the ground and unfastened a series of rawhide ties, and produced a long rifle from the package.

"I think Mingo's OK."Pardee said. "There's no blood on the horse or the saddle."

"I'd be mighty surprised if Mingo Perala allowed himself to get bushwhacked by some Yankee ranahans." Abel said as he checked the action on his Ross .303 calibre rifle. "I'm goin' to work my way up the creek bed to Mingo. You boys hightail it back down the trail a couple hundred yards and wait to hear from one of us."

"Barley." Abel looked at the young man now stuffing the pistol into a side pocket of his deerskin jacket, "they may be planning to hit us from the rear, so you lead the train back. If anybody tries to stop you, just open up with that handgun."

"You want me to shoot right at 'em?" Barley asked, eyes gleaming as he handed the reins of Abel's mare to Pardee and pulled himself up onto his horse.

"No... just a few rounds in the air to unsettle 'em." Abel said. "Them Montana boys usually don't have the stomach for taking fire; although they sure as hell like givin' it. If you come upon them, just make a lot of noise and stampede the train through 'em. They'll scatter." Abel tossed his canvas scabbard to Pardee.

Barley dallied the lead mule's halter rope around his saddle horn and turned animals on the narrow trail, leading them back down the mountain road. Pardee mounted up and leading Mingo's buckskin and Abel's roan, and followed the train back down the trail.

Abel sidled through the young poplars in the dry creek bed. Holding his rifle close to his chest, he made his way to a point parallel to where he estimated Mingo would have gone to ground. Then he began to work his way up the wooded slope.

The narrow mountain road, that led south to Chief Mountain and wound its way around official border crossings, was a favourite route of Canadian whiskey smugglers. Abel slowly followed a course parallel to the trail before he squatted and imitated the chuckling call of a Whiskey Jack. After a short interval his call was answered and he made his way toward his friend's location.

He parted the branches of a low-hanging poplar and saw Mingo's canvas duster visible through a stand of wolf willows. He smiled and was about to step forward when he felt cold steel against his neck.

"Git yer hands in the air, an' drop thet raffle." A voice whispered.

Abel raised his left hand then slowly bent his right knee and lowered his rifle allowing it to fall softly to the forest floor.

"Turn around, Mormon."

As Abel turned around to face his assailant his eyes widened in recognition.

"Freddie Hafner!"

"Hee hee hee ... " Freddie almost danced with glee. "I bet you never 'spected to set yore eyes on my face agin... did ye?"

"No, I sure didn't Freddie." Abel said as he examined the man before him. Freddie wore a wide-brimmed hat that cast his sunken eyes and long sallow face into shadow. He wore a long canvas duster over a vest that featured a silver deputy sheriff's badge. His striped woolen pants were tucked into high cut riding boots.

"Careful with that gun Freddie. You got no grounds to hold me up. That tin star ain't worth jack on this side of the border."

"Yeah," Freddie said, "How about that pack train a' booze yer drivin'?"

"Until that train crosses the border," Abel said. "No law has been broken. So put up that gun and stand down." Abel took a step in Freddie's direction."

"Oh, no ya don't." Freddie gripped his weapon tighter. "Yer stayin' put until th' Prophet gits over the border with yer sister..." Freddie paused and grimaced, "Ooh shit." He said, realizing his gaffe.

"My sister? What about ..." Abel's question was interrupted by the sound of gunfire and a man's scream from up the ridge. With Freddie's attention diverted, Abel grabbed the barrel of the rifle. Gripping it with both hands he pointed it skyward and simultaneously brought a knee up into Freddie's groin. Freddie squealed, relinquished the rifle, and grabbed his crotch in both hands. In an almost leisurely fashion, Abel swung the rifle around and butt-stroked Freddie on the jaw causing the man to go limp and collapse to the ground.

Abel looked down at the unconscious man before retrieving the Ross and Freddie's Winchester. Then, with a weapon in either hand, he made his way up the slope. He passed a piece of burlap, which he had taken to be Mingo's coat, and shook his head. "I'm losin' my touch," he said to himself as he sprinted to the poplars that populated the upper reaches of the valley.

Mingo, who was holed up behind a large Ponderosa pine, looked up as Abel quietly moved up beside him.

"What kept ya," he said as he raised his rifle and fired a shot that reverberated through the valley. "One a' them is holed up under that outcrop," Mingo said as he jacked another round into his weapon.

"Sounds like you got a piece a' one of them." Abel said.

"Yeah, the one that was holed up to my left. The pot lickers tried to suck me into a crossfire but they got a few things to learn about enfilading fire."

"If we had the time we could outwait them," Abel said. But Freddie let it slip that the Prophet has Faith. It looks to me like these guys are supposed to pin us down while the Prophet gets away with her."

Mingo's shoulders slumped and he shook his head sorrowfully. "I shoulda known they was up to something. They waited until we made a whiskey run then they went in and grabbed her when she was visiting her mother." He looked at Abel. "What d'ya want to do?"

"Freddie Hafner is out there havin' a noonday nap and he's goin' to be out fer awhile so I got to get aholt a' one of these bastards and make him tell us what route the Prophet is taking to the border. After all these years, that son of a bitch is still a burr under my saddle. I thought he had finally given up on Faith."

"Can you believe that sumbitch Hafner?" Mingo said.

"Yeah," Abel said, "he sticks to us like shit to a Hudson Bay blanket. Well ... let's find out if the one you hit is still alive. If he's able to talk we'll just pop the other one and be on our way. You lay down some covering fire to keep his head down and I'll go over to the left and see what's left of the bird you shot."

Both men took the time to load their weapons and, when Abel was ready to venture from cover, Mingo began laying down a steady stream of fire on the remaining gunman's position. The other man went to ground rather than return fire and Abel used the time to work his way from tree to tree until he came upon a blood trail, which he followed to the body of a man curled up in a fetal position. Abel knelt beside the body and tugged at the man's shoulder rolling him over. The tear-streaked face of Erwin Hafner turned to look at him.

"Yer in bad shape Erwin. You tell me which trail the Prophet is on and I'll have the boys take you back to Pincher. You don't. I'll leave you here for the bears and cougars to gnaw on."

"He's going straight to Bug Mountain." Erwin volunteered readily. "On the trail under the Chief."

"You better not be shitting me Erwin, 'cause if you are, I'll come looking for ya."

Erwin shook his head. "He's takin' the Chief Mountain trail." Abel felt a wave of pity for this damaged man, who was constantly being led astray by his brother.

Abel cupped a hand around his mouth and shouted. "It's OK Mingo, I've got what I need."

One final shot rang out. Then silence.

When Pardee and Barley arrived with the mules, Mingo instructed them to cache the liquor, bury the dead gunman, deliver Freddie to the police and take Erwin to Pincher for medical attention. Within minutes of issuing the order, Abel and Mingo were mounted and galloping south.

Familiar with the little-known trail that the Prophet was using, Mingo and Abel executed a series of shortcuts that led them to a position below and across the river from the trail. They forded the river, scaled the escarpment, and gained the trail some twenty minutes ahead of the oncoming riders.

Finding a strategic location, at a point where the trail wound close to the edge of the cliff, they dismounted and rested their tired horses. They loosened saddle girths and allowed the heaving animals to cool off while they planned their strategy.

Abel removed a pair of field glasses from a saddlebag and scanned the mountainous terrain. He played the binoculars over the landscape and then stopped.

"Five riders. Looks like the Prophet in the lead, then Faith, and three others behind them."

"How do you want to play this?" Mingo asked, taking the glasses from Abel and observing the riders.

"I'll ride out and face him. You cover me from here. If one of those black hats makes a move, show him the error of his ways. Remember that these bastards can't be allowed to go back to their settlement and bring a posse after us. This son of a bitch has done no end of harm to my family, but it ends here."

Mingo nodded, jacked a round into his

Winchester, and took up a position under the lower boughs of a pine tree. They waited until the oncoming riders emerged from a forested depression and proceeded towards them. When they were within 30 yards, Abel tightened the cinch on his saddle, mounted up and nudged his horse out onto the trail.

The lead rider, mounted on a handsome Appaloosa, was nodding in his saddle. His chin bobbed in concert with the horse's gait.

"Abel!" The sound of Faith's voice wakened the man and he blinked his eyes at the mounted man on the trail ahead of him.

Abel noted that the riders had quickly closed ranks around his sister while the Prophet brought his mount to a halt and sat staring at Abel, his eyes glowing from under his wide-brimmed Stetson.

"Well nephew. I don't know from whence you sprang ... but I would suggest that you back away if..."

"If I know what's good for me?" Abel grinned and urged his mount forward until he was stirrup to stirrup with the man.

"Japheth!" The Prophet snapped his fingers and one of the riders unholstered a pistol and made to draw a bead on Abel. Mingo's rifle barked and the man's hat flew back off of his head. His eyes bugged out and he dropped his gun, turned his mount around and galloped off. A second rider raised a rifle but felt a bullet pluck at his collar and let the weapon fall to the ground before also taking flight. The third man needed no further incentive to send him on his way. He spun his horse around and joined his companions in a hasty retreat.

When the confusion and tumult subsided Abel noticed that the Prophet was training a snub nose British Bulldog revolver at Faith.

"Back off Abel," the man said, "or your sister is dead"

Abel launched himself from his saddle, grabbed the Prophet and carried him off of his horse. Both men landed on the ground at the Appaloosa's feet. Spooked, the animal reared up and brought his front hooves down on Abel's back. The movement pushed both men to the lip of the gorge and, as he slid to the edge, Abel gripped a tree root and, with his free arm, pushed his adversary over the edge. The man fell from the heights of the cliff, bounced off an outcropping, and then fell to the rock-strewn river below.

Faith sat her horse paralyzed with shock as Mingo ran up and reached out to pull his friend from the lip of the gorge. Abel looked up, shook his head and whispered: "I'm done for old friend." Looking up at Faith he said, "I love you Little Sister," before relinquishing his hold on the root and falling to the streambed below.

※　　※　　※

Mingo and Faith, who was sixteen at the time, spent two days riding to Pincher Creek. Faith led her brother's horse, his Ross rifle in its saddle scabbard, while Mingo led the Prophet's Appaloosa with Abel's body tied to it.

They had ridden down to the river and recovered Abel's body. While Mingo secured Abel to the Prophet's horse -- he spared Abel's mare from the sad duty -- Faith spotted the Prophet's body, face down in the water. She kicked it free and watched it float away with the current.

On the long ride back, Faith told Mingo that Japheth, one of the Prophet's henchman, and the man for whom she had been selected, told her that it was God's will that they were to marry and he would track her and find her if she ran away again. One of the other riders had joked,

"If she gets away an' gets married in a church and has her cherry broken, she'll be rid a' ya. "

"Well," said Japheth. "We all know that ain't gonna happen. She's mine fer good now."

The Prophet's followers had spooked Faith and she felt she had to find someone to marry in order to prevent Japheth from tracking her down. When she mentioned it to Mingo, he chuckled.

"I'll bet there are hundreds of likely lads who would love to land up with a beautiful girl like you. Christ. I'd marry you... just to put yer mind at rest, but I'm spoken for."

Faith smiled ruefully: "Moira wouldn't take it kindly if you married me."

"Fraid she wouldn't." Mingo said.

Willie Shingoose and his brothers met them several miles from Pincher Creek and took Abel's body for burial on the reserve. Faith and Mingo rode to the mounted police detachment at Pincher Creek and detailed the events on Bug Mountain.

Because the incident had transpired in Montana, the events south of the line were outside of Mountie jurisdiction, Sergeant Halliday wrote a cursory account of the events and filed it away. When Mingo asked about the Hafner brothers, Halliday told him that Erwin was in the hospital and expected to recover. Freddie had been escorted to the border, where he was released. Before they left the detachment, Halliday said: "Oh, I almost forgot. I have something for you Mingo."

He went into a back room and emerged with a package. "This was in your saddle bag. It was recovered on the field at Moreuil and it found its way here."

Mingo recognized the package as the one Callum Fraser had given him prior to the action at Moreuil Wood.

After Abel's funeral, Faith and Mingo caught a train for Edmonton. He had a promise to fulfill and she wanted to be as far from Bug Mountain as possible.

Malcolm Fraser had been overjoyed with the package of 'French postcards' that his younger son had purchased for him. He was so thankful at Mingo's kindness that -- when he heard the cowboy was looking for a place to raise and train horses -- offered the big cowboy a twenty-acre parcel at half the going price. Never having owned any land, Mingo made the purchase and was soon clearing an area for a cabin and some corrals.

Part Two

Chapter 6 – Calder Boys

Edmonton, Alberta, August 1927

AFTER ACCOMPANYING MINGO TO HIS ACREAGE and getting acquainted with his uncle's horses, Billy began exploring the area around the property. Discovering a path leading into a forested area, he followed it and sampled berries and smelled flowers that were new to him. After some time spent walking, the tops of his new boots began to chafe his legs and he stopped to tuck his pant legs into them. Then, pushing back his hat he resumed his journey. He was picking gooseberries when he felt something prod him in the back. Turning, he was surprised by the sight of a small boy with a painted face glowering at him. The boy brandished a tree branch whittled to resemble a spear.

"Yer my prisoner Redcoat."

"Your prisoner?" Billy laughed. "Who are you supposed to be?"

"I'm Uncas an' yer my prisoner.

"Uncas, eh? Then you must be the Last of the Mohicans."

The boy gave him a blank look and said: "I'm taking you to see Hawkeye."

"That's good," Billy said. "I've always wanted to meet Hawkeye.

The boy led him to a cabin that was almost obscured by forest growth. Behind the structure a number of boys, made up to look like frontiersmen and Indians, were converting hockey sticks into long rifles. Billy smiled. He looked forward to playing with such inventive boys.

"Who you got there, Peewee...Hoot Gibson?" A boy, wearing a passable rendition of a coonskin hat, said.

"He ain't no cowboy." Peewee said. He's a Redcoat."

"Well, then. You better take him to Hawkeye."

"That's I'm doin'." Peewee said testily.

Inside the windowless cabin Peewee conducted Billy to another coonskin-capped boy, who was lighting a roll-your-own from the open end of the glass chimney of a kerosene lamp. Puffing the cigarette into life, the boy turned around.

"What's up, Peewee?" He said.

"He's a British spy. I found him lurkin' in the bush."

"The boy turned to Billy. "What you got to say fer yerself. Mr. Tom Mix?"

"My name is not Tom Mix. It's Billy."

"Billy," Peewee chimed in. "Maybe he's Billy the Kid."

"Billy the Hick is more like it." Hawkeye said.

Billy found the remark hurtful and he took an involuntary step backward, bumping into Peewee, who once again poked him in the back with his makeshift spear. He whirled on the boy, grabbed the spear and broke it over his knee. The boy began to cry. "You broke my spear you bastard."

"What didya do that for?" Hawkeye asked.

"That little bugger stabbed me once too often. And, besides, I don't like taking crap from some poser with a dead cat on his head."

Hawkeye stared at him for a moment, then pointed to the door.

"Well, there's the door. Don't let it hit you on the ass." He paused, searching for a suitable appellation. Then added:

"Hayseed."

Billy stormed out of the cabin, pushing his way through several boys gathered at the doorway. He made for the path and followed it back to the Fraser house. Halfway down the trail he realized that someone in the trees was travelling a parallel course to the path he was following.

"All right Peewee, I see you there. C'mon out."

He heard a rustling sound and decided to confront his stalker. He stepped off of the path and found himself staring into the large brown eyes of a small, tanned girl. The girl, a chubby waif of four of five, turned and ran into the forest.

Billy wondered what strange world he had entered? He had read about forest elves called Brownies. Had he just seen one? And those boys. They seemed like something out of Peter Pan. The Wild Boys. He closed his eyes and shook his head. Then he resolutely marched down the path away from the make believe Indians and Brownies.

That evening at supper, Billy finally met Deke, who turned out to be Hawkeye. They wordlessly shook hands when Faith introduced them, and sat quietly eating their food as Faith tried to make conversation. Ewan was on a freight run and Mingo had business with Moira in Winnipeg so neither was present to help dispel the tension in the room.

"I must say. You boys don't have much to say to each other."

"Mm hmph." Deke mumbled through a mouthful of bread. Billy remained silent.

"Well, it's been a long day for you Billy. How was the train ride?"

"Good."

"Derek, did you go fishing at the Sturgeon today?"

"Nope."

"Oh, this is ridiculous. You boys go outside. I'll clean up."

Two boys were seated on the steps of the veranda as Deke and Billy walked out of the house.

"Hey Deke. Want to play some ball? Everybody's at the field."

"Sure," Deke said. "I'll go get my glove."

Ignoring Billy, the trio made for an open field adjacent to the Fraser property. Billy could see and hear a number of boys welcome Deke as he joined them. He had spent a lot of time alone and had put up with Gus's meanness for almost a year. But this rejection -- by kids his own age -- stung, and he felt a pang of something akin to physical pain as the sounds of the ball game reached him.

Deke and his friends ostracized him for the remaining week of summer vacation. Billy would rise early in order to avoid Deke who usually slept in, and walk to Mingo's acreage to spend the day with his uncles' horses. Buster had arrived from Saskatchewan and Billy spent the days attempting to win back the horse's friendship.

For her part, Faith was perplexed by the complete lack of chemistry between the boys. Boys, who she had hoped, would become the best of friends. She watched sadly as Billy left for Mingo's place every morning while Deke's friends would appear and accompany him on any adventure he would devise for them.

On the first day of school -- Faith had preregistered Billy when she heard that he was coming to Edmonton -- she insisted that Deke accompany Billy to and from school and he wordlessly complied. He directed Billy to his homeroom, helped with his orientation, and came for him at the end of the school day.

As they were taking a short cut down an alley, on that first day of school, they were accosted by a group of older boys.

"Hey Tonto," a beefy boy, with a face covered in angry acne, addressed Deke. "Melvin Mandryk tole me you got some Injun blood in ya."

Deke's shoulders tensed and, in an aside to Billy, he murmured: "Keep your eyes down and keep walkin'."

"What's going on?" Billy said. Before Deke could answer, the boy stepped in front of them and pushed a finger into Deke's chest. "Hey Wagon Burner, I'm talkin' to you."

"Screw you Callander." Deke hissed through clenched teeth.

"What was that?" Callander said, cupping a hand to his ear. "What did you say?"

"I said. Screw you Callander."

"That's what I thought you said." Callander said, and punched Deke in the mouth, sending the smaller boy hurtling backwards. Billy rushed to Deke, who was struggling to his feet, and blocked him from the view of Callander, who was being congratulated by his cronies. He pushed an object into Deke's hand and Deke whistled in appreciation at the sight of the brass knuckles that rested in his palm.

"Quick," Billy urged. "Put them on." Deke obliged and with Billy's help, regained his feet.

"Hey Callander," Deke shouted to the bully, who was walking away with his cronies. "You chicken liver piece of shit. I ain't through with you."

Callander stopped, and after a moment's hesitation, turned and made for Deke, who stood sideways with his armoured right hand coiled behind him. When the bully was within striking range, Deke's fist snaked out and punched him in the forehead.

The boy stopped in his tracks. His eye's rolled back and he drunkenly swayed on his feet allowing Deke to strike again. This time his right hand landed on the point of Callander's chin dropping him to his knees.

When Callander had charged Deke, it appeared that the remaining boys were prepared to be spectators until one of them, a skinny kid known as "Spitter" Smattello, decided to earn some kind of peer group credibility and came after Billy.

Billy soon realized that the 'Spitter' came by his nickname honestly as a mist of saliva sprayed from the boy's mouth as he spoke.

"And who are you?" he sneered. "The breed's girlfriend?" Spitter swaggered, milking the moment. Billy took the time to mentally review the boxing moves Gus had taught him. Then he raised his fists and turned sideways to his meet his adversary.

Spitter, who stood almost a head taller than Billy, rocked his shoulders back and forth with a confident air.

"Haw... haw... haw. Lookit this poser." Spitter crowed. "Thinks he's Jack Dempsey."

With his opponent's hands hanging down, Billy moved in and hit Spitter with two quick left jabs. The second blow opened Spitter's upper lip and the following right cross, flattened his nose. With a split lip and blood coursing down his face,

Spitter began to blubber and, spitting blood, held his hands up in surrender.

That should have ended it. But three members of Callander's band of thugs were Smatellos, a pair of twins and Spitter. The twins tackled Billy from behind.

"Fall down you goddamn ox." Deke said, as he was about to deliver a *coup de gras* to Callander. When he saw that Billy was being pummeled by the Smatellos he came up behind one of them and rapped him on the back of the head. The boy yelped and retreated. Then, Billy and Deke stood back to back and discouraged any further combat.

"Know, what I'm gonna call you from now on?" Deke grinned, his tongue rubbing a chipped tooth. "Billy the Fightin' Finn."

Chapter 7 – The Night Prowler

Fraser Residence October 1932

Near midnight a grey-muzzled German Shepherd with one lazy ear rose to his haunches and raised a hue-and-cry. Chained to a stake in front of his doghouse, Bomber was smart enough not to attempt to outrun the length of his tether so he compensated by barking loud enough to wake everyone in the house. He was gratified when a window on the second-floor slid open but his anticipation was short-lived when a woman's voice admonished him to cease and desist. He uttered a frustrated, rumbling growl, turned and retreated into his sleeping quarters where he dropped to his stomach and rested his chin on his outstretched paws.

In the morning two boys, armed with .22 rifles, approached Bomber's abode. One boy dropped to his knees, hugged the dog and scratched him behind the ears while the animal danced at the prospect of being released from his confinement.

"Hey Bomber, you goofy old wolf dog. What were you yellin' about last night?"

"Hey Deke, look at this." Billy was standing by the caragana hedge that enclosed the backyard. He pointed to a coloured fabric caught in the spiky branches of the hedge. Closer examination revealed it to be a woolen scarf wrapped around several broken eggs. Now convinced of the existence of a nocturnal prowler, Deke and Billy began to formulate plans to capture the culprit. They spent that day following Bomber around the property, hoping he would pick up the trail. Unfortunately, Bomber was more of a watchdog than a tracker and they called off the search at suppertime.

Faith was not enthusiastic about the boys staging a confrontation with someone who could possibly do them some harm, or vice versa, so she confiscated their firearms and grounded them for the evening.

"It was probably just someone looking for something to eat," she said, "Someone who was too shy, or proud, to ask at the door. No one should be penalized for being hungry. I'm going to leave some food on the veranda tonight."

"Are you crazy?" Deke said. "You feed that bum and he'll never leave. Let me unchain Bomber and let him run off whoever is lurking around."

Faith whirled on him, "You watch your tongue mister ... and get rid of that snotty attitude. If you would let me finish my sentence ... I'm betting that the food I set out will not be touched. I am sure that this... this... visitor has continued on his way. He's probably at the Calder yard right now trying to catch a freight to the coast. I want you to bring Bomber into the house tonight because I don't want him mauling anybody. You boys are not to leave the house. You have to get an early start in the morning. Mingo is coming home tomorrow and he'll expect to have his potato patch weeded and his horses fed and watered."

Faith was nervous about the prowler and she wanted Bomber and the boys in the house in case someone was lurking around outside.

Billy watched as Deke's face tightened into a scowl as he bolted from the room. Faith had Deke on a short leash and the boy had trouble reining in his short temper in exchanges with her. He often confided in Billy that she hated him and he didn't know why. For his part, Billy was very uncomfortable with any criticism of Faith. Deke was his best friend but Faith held a special place in his heart. She had unconditionally accepted him as part of her family when his uncle brought him to Edmonton.

Mingo had built a small cabin and several corrals on his twenty-acre holding. Like a lot of combat veterans, he had devils to cope with and he found that working with horses offered him a modicum of serenity. His wartime experience had burdened him with guilt over his part in sending so many horses to agonizing ends. In atonement, he began to devote his time to gentling outlaws

-- animals who refused to yield to servility -- that he purchased from farmers and ranchers who had given up on them. Problem horses usually ended up at the wrong end of a rifle barrel at a mink ranch or a glue factory, but Mingo did his best to save a number of them.

He had a life long affinity for horses and spent hours transforming the equine rejects into gentle saddle and carriage horses. From time to time, he also worked with heavy horses, which were in demand in an area where horse transportation still rivaled automobiles. He made every effort to place his charges in good hands but on the few occasions that someone mistreated a horse, they received a prompt refund with the horse being summarily repossessed.

Before Malcolm left for Scotland, he gave Mingo the formula for TLT, the valuable potable mixture that bootleggers like Ozzie Callander purchased by the gallon. For that reason Mingo always planted several acres of potatoes, which the boys were charged with weeding and watering.

After their evening meal Faith left the boys in front of the Philco console radio, and repaired to the kitchen. She filled a ceramic bowl with sandwiches and cookies and covered it with a dishtowel. She left it on the steps of the veranda beside a pint bottle of milk. The following morning, the empty milk bottle sat next to the bowl, now empty except for the neatly folded dishtowel.

Evidence of a prowler now being conclusive, moved Deke to suggest to Billy that the skulker be run off or, if possible, captured. That Saturday morning, as the boys followed Bomber over the dirt road that led to Mingo's place, Deke knew that Billy's respect for Faith would make him difficult to enlist, so he advanced an argument that convinced Billy to cooperate. The prowler could be some kind of a sex fiend who was after Faith.

That night, armed with baseball bats and a flashlight -- their rifles remained locked away -- Bomber and the boys were stationed in the hayloft of the old barn. They waited for almost two hours and were about give up, when Deke grabbed Billy's arm and pointed toward the house. It was a moonless night but they could make out a shadowy figure moving against the white background of the veranda. They dropped from the loft and made for the house. Deke ran up and engaged the visitor, an action that triggered an outburst of screaming and swearing.

"Let me go you bastard! I swear... I'll kill you."

Billy was surprised that the voice was high pitched and not that of an adult. He illuminated the scene with the flashlight and saw Deke grappling with a small boy who was giving him all he could handle. The little guy was in constant motion, with arms swinging and feet kicking.

"Billy!" Deke yelled. "Give me a bloody hand."

Billy dropped the flashlight and wrapped his arms around the prowler's upper body but the boy's lower extremities remained free and he caught Deke with a kick to a sensitive area of his anatomy.

At that point the porch light came on and Faith stepped out on to the veranda.

"What on earth is all the racket?" She demanded. "Stop it! This minute!"

Billy relinquished his hold on the small figure and Deke limped away to walk off the pain inflicted by his pint-sized adversary.

Faith stepped down onto the front walk and picked up Billy's flashlight. She approached the boy, who hadn't moved, and removed the large tweed cap that obscured his face. She raised the light.

"And who might you be?"

"It's Rosie Callander," Deke volunteered.

"Rosie?" Faith said peering closely at the child. "A girl?'"

Rosie was the daughter of Ozzie Callander, the bootlegger who ran a blind pig operation north of the city limits near Turnip Lake. Known as The Compound, it was a collection of ramshackle buildings that provided a venue for drinkers, gamblers and those who partook of the whores Ozzie employed.

As Faith pressed Rosie for answers, the girl admitted that she had been sleeping in the Hideout -- a statement that evinced a scowl from Deke -- and was preparing to catch a freight train to British Columbia where she could live on a beach.

"You'll do nothing of the sort young lady, I'm going to take you home to your father." Mention of her father caused the girl to turn and attempt to break away. Faith caught her and, gripping her by the shoulders, brought her under the porch light.

She noticed that tears were streaming down the girl's cheeks and she began to gently cajole the child into telling her what had caused her to live like a hobo and hide out in a shack in the bush.

Rosie explained why she was running away. School was set to resume and she had no intention of going back to be treated like trash by the kids and the teachers because of her father's reputation and her threadbare wardrobe. Then, the little girl divulged the main reason for her escape. Several times, during the child's discourse, Faith had gasped audibly, especially when she heard the child had recently been returned to her father after her aunt, Ozzie's sister, who had cared for the girl, from the ages of four to ten, had died. Ozzie took her back, realizing that she was old enough to work in the kitchen and serve drinks. Rosie soon realized that she had to have her wits about her and move fast to avoid the attentions of some of the drunks.

Rosie spent six weeks in her father's service until an incident with a patron convinced her of a need to escape. Several nights before, a man had grabbed her and was dragging her into the bush when her brother Chance had caught up with them. Chance had beaten the man senseless with a sawed-off pool cue, and then walked away without a word of comfort for his sister.

The morning after the attempted assault, Rosie filled a pillowcase with a small ham, several loaves of bread, a number of apples and several bottles of Coca Cola. Taking care not to wake the habitués of the Compound, she slipped out of a back door and made her way south toward the city limits.

When she entered the forest, redolent with late-summer aroma of high bush cranberries, she felt at ease and in her element. She walked for several hours, stopping from time to time to collect some saskatoons in her cap. After almost an hour, she came upon a path that diverged from the main trail. She had followed it to a small cabin that was almost hidden in the trees that surrounded it.

From the time she could confidently navigate on her own two feet, Rosie had roamed these woods. Six years ago, she had watched, from cover, when Deke Fraser, Mitch Pawluk and several other boys had built the cabin -- from materials purloined from the Calder rail yard -- and dubbed it The Hideout. She had been four at the time and remembered envying the boys because they not only had each other but, at the end of the day, they could go home to parents who cared about them. Rosie had never known her mother; she had been in the care of Ozzie's sister, until the woman's death left the ten-year old in the care of an uncle that wanted no part of raising a child and promptly returned her to her father.

Billy, Deke and their cronies had spent most of the summer looking after Mingo's place as Mingo had spent most of the late summer with Moira. In his absence, the boys were charged with feeding and watering his animals and weeding his potato patch. They had the run of his cabin and outbuildings and christened the twenty-acre spread, Shiloh, after the ranch in The Virginian, which, together with The Last of the Mohicans, were Deke's favourite novels. They were given permission to ride some of Mingo's saddle horses, which made that summer memorable for the Calder boys.

Before her traumatic experience at The Compound, Rosie had discovered that the Hideout didn't enter into the boys' plans for the summer and, when she needed to escape it would be a safe place to hole up. No one at the Compound, including Chance, knew of her hiding place. When she arrived at the cabin, she found the door had been fastened with a CNR padlock, but she knew where the switch key, which opened it, was hidden.

She spent several days in the dark, windowless structure reading the boys' collection of comics; cloth bound adventure novels and Big Little books by lamplight. She enjoyed herself, until her provisions ran out. With her food sack empty, she moved further south and prowled the Fraser property. She discovered several crab apple trees and filled her hat with the fruit and drank from the pump. She had decided that she would harvest enough apples, and maybe some eggs, to see her to the rail yard, where she could catch ride a boxcar to the coast.

Faith interrupted the girl's story. "Didn't Bomber bother you?"

"Bomber and I are old pals." Rosie said, reaching out to pat the dog. When he's free to roam on his own, we go exploring."

"Hey, that's our dog." Deke said.

"He's Mingo's dog." Billy said. "And he wouldn't mind." Rosie smiled at Billy and continued. "Bomber did make a fuss last night though."

"I think Ozzie sent somebody to find me," the girl said. "I hid in the doghouse and Bomber scared off whoever it was."

"How come you hid if it was somebody from your place?" Deke said.

"Cuz, I'm never goin' back there. If you try to take me there, I'll just run away again."

Faith took Rosie into the kitchen, cleaned her face and hands, poured her a glass of milk and made her a peanut-butter sandwich. She stood quietly for several moments and then pronounced.

"From now on Rosie, you are going to live here with us."

"What about Ozzie?" The girl asked anxiously.

"Leave that to me." Faith left the kitchen and walked out onto the veranda where the boys were discussing the surprising turn of events. They looked up when Faith approached them.

"How dare you boys set a trap for that poor little soul. As if she didn't have enough problems, she had to be attacked by a couple of self-appointed vigilantes."

Deke scowled but Billy was genuinely hurt by the tone of her voice. She quizzed the boys about Rosie's situation. Billy knew of the girl's existence, but knew little else. Deke, who had a number of gossipy friends, corroborated a good part of the girl's story.

Faith stood quietly for several moments, then,

having made a decision, said: "Derek, will you go in and keep Rosie company? Billy, you come with me."

Deke demanded to know why he had to stay. Faith turned to him and said, "You scare me witless when you drive. Billy is a good driver. Besides someone has to keep an eye on Rosie. I don't want her running off."

That didn't sit well with Deke but Faith had no more time for him. Ewan had taken pains to teach both boys to drive because he considered Faith's driving to be life threatening. She walked briskly to the Essex, which was parked in an old machine shed.

Once behind the wheel he turned to her. "Where are we going?"

"To the Callander compound.

"Really?" Billy said.

"Really." Faith confirmed. "Start this jalopy and let's go."

Billy was a sturdy boy of thirteen who could handle himself. However, the prospect of going against Chance Callander, who had grown into a hulking brute since their encounter some years earlier, would be a little scary without the support of his best friend. He took a deep breath, flipped on the ignition switch and stepped on the floor-mounted starter button. The engine surged to life and, as he backed it out of the building, he made a silent oath not to let Faith down. Whatever it took.

Chance had quit school shortly after the now

famous Jurva/Fraser versus Callander/Smatello encounter of 1927. He wasn't of legal age to quit but no one; administrators, teachers or students, wanted him back and a case of truancy was never pressed. Ozzie didn't mind that his son had left school; he was happy to have a fulltime, unpaid hand at the Compound. Deke and Billy had been anointed local heroes after that famous brawl but neither of them had had subsequent dealings with Chance.

The car moved easily on the gravel street known as City Limit Road, but when it encountered the muddy dirt road, which led north to the Compound, Billy had to fight to keep the big car from sliding off the road or getting mired in the series of water-filled potholes that dotted the road as a result of the previous day's rainstorm. He was actually relieved when the lights of the compound came in sight. He turned the car at the gateway and followed the muddy ruts that led into the yard, bringing the Essex to a sliding stop in front of the main building.

Faith reached over and honked the horn and Billy almost swooned as one of her breasts accidently rubbed against the back of his hand. She kept honking the horn until Chance Callander, dressed in a pair of long johns and high-top rubber boots, came out and stood under a porch light. He opened a button on his underwear and urinated from the porch into a mud puddle before cupping a hand over his eyes attempting to identify the occupants of the Essex. "Who the hell are you and what do you want?"

"I want to talk to Mr. Callander. I want to talk to him now!"

"Ozzie ain't here..." Chance spat a stream of brown tobacco spittle into the same puddle. "What'ya want?"

"It is a crime how Rosie is being treated here." Faith raised her voice. "I'm not going to stand for it. You tell your father that your sister is now in my care. I will contact the authorities if I don't hear from him.

Without warning, a naked woman emerged from the doorway behind Chance. She stepped down from the elevated wooden walkway that connected the buildings, and staggered toward the car with a drink in one hand, a cigarette in the other. She sipped her drink as she weaved her way into the island of light created by the headlights.

Billy froze, forgetting to breathe. It was first time he had seen a naked woman illuminated by bright lights. His eyes fastened on her as she walked to the front of the car and shouted.

"Who the hell do you think you are?" She held a finger aloft. "Wait... Don't tell me ... I've heard of you. You're the one who thinks she's the second coming of Queen Victoria."

"You shut up. You bitch!" Billy yelled, incensed that anyone would speak to Faith in such a manner. His foot slipped off of the clutch pedal and the Essex lurched ahead and stalled. The woman dropped her drink and extended her hands to protect herself and fell backwards into a large mud puddle.

"Billy you stay in the car!" Faith said as she exited the vehicle. But, Billy was already outside. Faith went to the mud-covered woman, who had risen to a sitting position and pulled her to her feet. "Billy, you keep your eyes to yourself and apologize this instant for calling this lady a name."

Billy mumbled an "I'm sorry," looking away from the woman.

When he looked again he saw that Faith had taken off her own sweater and wrapped it around the woman's waist.

"You don't have to live this way," Billy heard her tell the woman, whose shoulders were heaving. She looked at Faith for a moment with a sad look in her eyes, and then pulled away. "Screw you Lady Bountiful ... I don't need your advice ... or your pity. I'll have you know I was educated at McGill University and my family is worth more than this whole goddamned, flea-bitten city put together."

By then, clientele and staff had emerged from the various buildings to rubberneck. Chance and some of the men guffawed, but the women were silent as Faith helped the mud-covered woman climb the steps to the walkway. "Hey Baby," one man yelled at Faith. "I'd pay five dollars fer a piece a' yer ass." Another man told him to button his lip, unless he wanted to deal with Mingo Perala.

Walking to the passenger side of the car, Faith dropped into the seat and slammed the door. She shook her head slowly and Billy noticed then that she had a streak of mud on her cheek. She sighed deeply and said: "Let's get the hell out of here."

She didn't say anything for most of the drive home and Billy thought she was unhappy with him so he apologized for his behaviour. She looked over at him and smiled. "Thank you Billy, for coming to my defense like you did." She paused and giggled.

"I hope you're not going to be corrupted for life by the sight of that wild, mud covered floozy."

"N-no, I don't think so," Billy said, as she punched him lightly on the arm. "No. I'm sure I won't."

She sat back in silence for several moments, then said: "You know that I will not allow Rosie to go back there, don't you? If that ... that low-life bootlegger thinks he's getting her back, he has another think coming."

Back at the Fraser home, Billy pulled the Essex up to the front walk. Before she left the car, Faith turned to him, squeezed his arm and whispered. "Thanks again Billy."

With his heart swelling, Billy parked the car in the machine shed and walked to the house. Deke sat alone in the kitchen and Billy looked at him inquiringly, disappointed at Faith's absence.

"They're in the bathroom. Faith is gonna clean up the little shit. She wants us to fire up the sauna."

Being of Finnish extraction, Mingo was accustomed to having a steam bath close at hand and had constructed a sauna on his own acreage and one for the Frasers. Billy and Deke carried kindling and firewood from the woodpile and loaded it into the fieldstone-covered oil drum that functioned as a heater. They lit the kindling and, while the fire worked to heat the stones, they filled a wooden pail with cold water and placed it on the lower seating bench. They placed a metal dipper in the pail, left the sauna hut and withdrew to the house.

Faith and Rosie sat waiting in the kitchen. Rosie was wrapped in an adult-size bathrobe with only her face and disheveled hair visible. Faith had changed to a man's shirt and denim pants causing Billy to think that she too looked like a little kid.

"Give it a half-hour," Deke said, "and the rocks'll be hot enough to steam. I made some coffee. Want some?"

"That's great Derek. Let's have some coffee. Billy, there's a tin of ginger snaps in the cupboard. Derek get the canned milk from the pantry and some lemonade from the ice box for Rosie."

"I drink coffee," the girl said.

Faith chuckled. "You are too young to drink coffee Missy."

"I'm almost eleven. I drink coffee all the time."

"I'm afraid that you'll just have to settle for lemonade, cocoa, or Postum."

"Postum!" Deke exclaimed. "Nobody drinks that stuff. It's made out of wheat straw and sawdust."

"Oh, it is not." Faith laughed. "Would you like some cocoa, Rosie?" Rosie accepted cocoa as a compromise when Billy also opted for it.

After emerging from their session in the sauna, Faith and Rosie repaired to the bathroom where the girl luxuriated in warm, scented water while Faith shampooed her hair. Then, wrapped in a large bath towel, she sat on a kitchen chair while Faith cut and curled her damp tresses. The boys occupied themselves with the comic section of the Toronto Star Weekly.

The following day, Deke and Billy accompanied Faith and Rosie on a shopping spree in the city. Deke drove the Essex and waited with Billy outside of Eaton's and The Hudson Bay Company, while Faith picked out a new wardrobe for the girl.

Later that afternoon after the car, loaded with female paraphernalia, returned to the Fraser property, Rosie tried on some of her new outfits. Faith had the boys burn the girl's shirt, overalls and cloth cap in the barrel behind the barn.

Before Faith took her in hand, Rosie had been a tough little tomboy with a smart mouth and a vocabulary that would make a sailor blush. She had a hard-earned reputation for being able to whip any boy in her general size range and often gave better than she got against bigger kids. After Faith unveiled her protégé, no one would believe that this beautiful girl and the tough little scamp were the same person. Billy hit his forehead with the palm of his hand as he realized that this girl was the mysterious Brownie he had seen in the woods five years earlier.

Rosie's heart-shaped face was softened by her curled hair, which now fell softly to her shoulders instead of being pulled tightly back and hidden by a cap. Her large, almond shaped, brown eyes, were a striking feature after being liberated from the shadow of the ragged tweed cap.

Chapter 8- The Soiled Dove

Near Turnip Lake, Alberta- Summer 1933

AFTER SOME GUFFAWING AND JOSTLING THE boys formed a lineup at the cabin door. Chance Callander appeared in the doorway and beckoned to Deke.

"OK Fraser, you're the big ladies man. You get the first go." Chance exposed his brown, broken teeth in a grin. "The resta' ya' will haveta ride a wet deck."

Deke placed a quarter in Chance's palm and as he disappeared into the dark cabin Billy rode up on his bicycle and asked what was going on. The boys appeared reluctant to tell him.

As he moved up to the doorway, Chance stayed him with a hand against the bib of his overalls. "Hold it Jurva. Let's see the colour of yer money first. Then you'll have to wait yer ..."

"Jeezuz Christ ... Billy get in here. Pronto!" Deke's voice stopped Chance in mid sentence. "What the fuck is goin' on?" he said turning to peer inside. "Hey!" He made a futile grab at Billy as he entered the cabin. When his eyes adjusted to the gloom, Billy saw Deke crouched over a naked woman who was vomiting blood onto the rough wooden floor. The woman was on her stomach, on a collection of old car seats, and Deke held her shoulders as her body spasmed and shuddered.

"Jesus, Billy we gotta do something." Deke's eyes were wide and his voice shook. "I think she's croaking."

"What did you do to her?" Billy said.

"Jesus Christ Billy! I didn't touch her. Honest to God. When I came in she rolled over and started puking. We gotta do something."

Billy turned to see an ashen-faced Ihor Kovik standing among the boys who had crowded into the doorway to see what was happening.

"Ihor, take my bike and go find Mingo."

Ihor fled the cabin followed by Chance Callander who promptly disappeared into the underbrush. The boys spent twenty harrowing minutes until they heard the familiar sound of Mingo's truck making its way down the overgrown road toward the cabin. Soon, a shadow filled the sunlight doorway and the boys looked up and froze at the sight of Faith.

"Oh my God!" she said, a hand flying to her mouth. "What have you boys done?"

"She's dying, Faith. Please do something." Deke looked up fearfully. "You can give us shit later."

Faith dropped to her knees in front of the woman, who had finally stopped coughing. She produced a handkerchief and began wiping the woman's face. "Oh no," she whispered.

"What?" Deke demanded. "Is she dead?

"No, she isn't." Faith said and looked to Mingo who had entered the cabin.

"Can we get her to a hospital?"

"Maybe. But they'd take one look at her and see those marks on her arms and peg her for what she is, a drug-addicted whore. They wouldn't go out of their way to save her. The sanctimonious pot lickers."

"She," Faith's eyes narrowed as she glared at the males around her, "is a human being and we're not going to sit here like a bunch of simps and let her die. Mingo, take that door down and we'll lay her on it. Derek, find something to cover her. Billy, you go make some room in the back of your uncle's truck."

"Where ya taking her Faith?" Deke asked nervously.

"We're taking her home."

"Home?" Deke swallowed. "Home ... to our house?"

"No," she responded. "To the old folk's home. What the hell do you think?"

After the woman had been transported to the attic room in the Fraser house, Faith telephoned Doctor MacRorie, whose initial recommendation had been to make the woman as comfortable as possible and, with the help of some painkillers, let her slip away. Faith refused to be party to such a venture and demanded that the doctor provide her with a game plan to help the woman recover.

For the first week, the patient, Dara McNight, slept fitfully in the darkened room. When she would awaken for short periods of time Faith and Rosie would attempt to feed her soup, which she would usually spit out. Her condition deteriorated and Faith began to think that the woman would die.

She obtained some vitamin compounds, and sustenance, which could be administered intravenously. Dara was placed in restraints -- cloth strips securing her to the bed to prevent her from pulling out the tube -- and started on an intravenous drip.

One day Faith entered to find her patient awake and howling with rage. When she entered the room, Dara was straining against her restraints and screaming.

"You bitch ... you dirty rotten bitch," she gasped. "Untie me. Now! And give me something to straighten me out. You hear me? I need something to ease this fucking pain."

Faith ignored her demands, examined Dara's eyes with a penlight then wordlessly left the room. For several days Dara slept fitfully while medication and sustenance flowed into her body. One day - when the door opened to reveal Rosie balancing a bowl of soup on a tray, Dara became more vocal in her demand for drugs. Rosie juggled the tray onto one hand and flipped a wall switch bringing a ceiling-mounted fixture to life.

"Turn it off ... turn it off!" Dara screamed

closing her eyes. And turning her face away from the light.

Rosie sat the tray down on a small dresser and turned the switch off. Moving toward the bed she said. "Faith says you have to eat something. I brought you some soup."

"Shove the soup up your ass you little bitch. I need a hit of something. Go tell Mingo ... he can get me some stuff."

"Mingo's in Montreal with Moira. Besides, even if he was here, he wouldn't give you any drugs."

Dara changed her tack. "Please, Rosie. You have to help me. I can't stand this pain anymore. I need some snow."

"Snow?" Rosie said. "You mean dope ... don't you?"

"I don't care what you call it," the woman gasped. Just get me some. Go to your dad ... or your brother."

At that moment Faith entered the room and, stepping in front of the child, faced the woman.

"How dare you ask this child to get drugs for you."

Dara was tugging at her restraints and uttering a primal keening sound. Faith ushered Rosie out of the room, closed the door and knelt at the bedside.

"Goddammit Dara! You'll either walk out of here clean ... or they'll carry you out of this room and bury your sorry skeleton of a body in Potter's Field."

The woman stopped crying and looked up at

Faith. Her red-rimmed eyes opened wide and she was quiet for several moments. She inhaled raggedly. "I'm not going to be buried in any fucking Potter's Field. Get me that soup."

"Y'know Dara? Once we get you clean and healed up, we're going to have to do something about your ... fucking ... language!"

Deke and Billy were helping Mingo repair one of his corrals, when Deke spotted Ozzie Callander's Model B roadster churning up a big plume of dust on the dirt road that led to the Fraser property. They knew that Faith, Rosie and Dara were the only ones at the house.

"Oh shit!" Deke said as he ran toward his bicycle. "Get Mingo." Billy saw Deke hop on his bicycle and disappear into the trees followed closely by Bomber. Billy ran around the house to the pasture where his uncle was saddling a roan mare and told him what had happened. Mingo tightened the cinch on the saddle, dropped a stirrup from its perch on the horn, and climbed up.

"Get that bob wire for me will you Bill?"

Billy rushed to open the portion of the barbed wire fence that functioned as a gate and Mingo nudged his horse into a gallop and made for the Fraser house.

Billy hitched up the fence, grabbed his two-wheeler and pedaled as fast as he could in the direction of the Fraser house. By the time he arrived, Mingo was on the steps of the veranda where Chance Callander was restraining Deke. Ozzie was pounding on the door and demanding to be admitted. Bomber was chasing a screaming Spitter Smatello down the road.

Mingo pulled on Chance's shoulder, spun him around, and punched him in the stomach. The air seemed to leave Chance and Deke and Billy took the opportunity to immobilize him, twisting his arms behind his back.

The door opened and Faith appeared, brandishing her brother's vintage Ross rifle, but when she saw Mingo she pointed the barrel at the floor.

"Oi've no argument wiv you Mingow." Ozzie squawked.

"If you got an argument with her," Mingo pointed to Faith, "then you've got an argument with me."

"If you think that you're taking Rosie from here. You've got another think coming." Faith said.

"We'oh, she is my do'ah and oll. But you can keep 'er. I kime for my 'oor. I 'ear she's 'ealfy enough to go back ta work."

For a moment, a shocked silence prevailed. Then Faith pulled back the bolt of the Ross and levered a round into the chamber. She walked to Ozzie and said: "You... low... slimy... degenerate... excuse for a human being." She placed the gun barrel under his nose and the little Cockney's hands flew up and he swallowed repeatedly.

"M-Mingow," tell 'er she's for the Jimmy Naow (Cockney rhyming slang for jail) if she does it. He closed his eyes tightly as Faith raised the tip of the barrel and pressed it between his eyes.

"O.K. O.K." Ozzie said. "Oi'll leave and not bovver you agin. Jist put dine the rifo."

"Faith," Mingo said soothingly. "Nuthin' good can come of this. Put it down." Faith reluctantly lowered the weapon and Ozzie sagged with relief.

Mingo grabbed Ozzie by the collar with both hands. "If you ever come around here again ... or go near that poor women upstairs ... or Faith, or Rosie," he said in a low voice. I promise, I'll hunt you down and cut yer scrawny little chicken throat. Now, take that punk of a son of yers and clear the hell outta here."

Ozzie and Chance returned to their car and Rosie let out a yelp of relief.

Chapter 9 – The Fireball

Edmonton, Alberta: Autumn 1935

THE TORONTO JUNIOR TEAM -- IN crisp Maple Leaf uniforms -- skated onto the ice and began warming up. As the goaltender, it fell to Billy to lead his Calder Dukes onto the Edmonton Gardens ice surface. As his teammates trooped out behind him, he heard a collective sigh of disappointment from the crowd.

Although the Calder team had matching jerseys, many were faded and some no longer had the gothic 'C' that served as their emblem. Some of Billy's teammates had shin pads showing through holes in their stockings; few wore matching hockey pants, and some wore pants that were too small for them. Many had skates with knotted laces.

Ewan had read about the Toronto Juniors and their young phenom, Tommy 'Fireball' Flynn and began to prepare his team, with strenuous practices, to win the right to represent Edmonton.

The Toronto team had played junior teams in Manitoba and Saskatchewan and was about to commence an Alberta swing. Tournaments had been set up to provide adversaries for the eastern team and, after a grueling series of play-offs the Calder Dukes won the right to represent Edmonton.

Billy had been a last minute addition to the team as the regular goaltender had broken a wrist during a playoff game. Billy, who didn't normally play hockey, was drafted because Ewan admired his quick boxer's reactions and his proficience as a catcher in baseball.

Ewan wasn't behind the bench for the all-important game. He had taken his regular freight run to Jasper, well before the tournament, but a derailment had tied up the main line for almost a week, causing him to miss the game. Al Zelenak, another CN hog head, filled in for him.

The game started out badly for the Dukes. Before a minute had elapsed, the Fireball had potted three goals. After a timeout -- to allow Billy to settle down -- the Dukes tied it up with two goals from Deke and one from Mitch.

The game was scoreless for the middle period except when Deke beat the Toronto goaltender with a sizzling shot that knocked him into the goal. In the final period, Billy crouched in the crease and fixed his attention on the incoming puck carrier. He could see Deke attempting to catch up to the opposing player to thwart a shot on goal, but the forward -- who had skated through Billy's team as if they were pylons -- leaned into his shot, flexing his stick to wrist the puck at the goal just as Deke caught up to him.

Billy awoke sometime later to a circle of anxious faces looking down at him. As he floated up out of a swirling silence he could see that their mouths were moving but he couldn't hear what they were saying.

He opened his mouth and a pop in his ears signaled that his hearing had returned. He winced as a cacophony of sound assailed him.

"Billy, hey Billy... You O.K.?" He recognized Deke's voice.

"Billy", can you hear me?" Coach Zelenak said. How you feelin?'

"I'm O.K., I think." He attempted to sit up.

"Don't do that!" The coach restrained him with a hand on his chest. "I sent one a' the boys to fetch the sawbones. You lie still 'til he gets here."

They kept Billy on his back until Doc MacRorie arrived, shone a light into each of his eyes, and brusquely pronounced him free of brain damage. That was if, he muttered, hockey players had brains to damage.

Billy's teammates helped him to his feet and he cursed when his exploring fingers encountered a large bump on his forehead.

"Jeez, my head is killin' me. Just exactly what the hell happened?"

"Aw," the coach drawled. "The son of a bitch rang a shot off of yer bean and cold cocked ya. You scared the shit outta us when you hit the ice and laid there like a pile a hoor's underwear."

"Really?" said Billy. "Did I make the save?"

"Nah, sorry kid. The prick potted the rebound."

"So we lost."

"Well, not really. The game is forfeit because of the brawl."

"Christ," Billy said. "I missed everything. I was entitled to a shot at the guy. What was his number?"

"Aw, it's that big star everybody's braggin' about. The one they call the Fireball." Coach Zelenak said. "If it's any consolation, Deke tuned him up purty good. After he beaned you, and scored the goal, Deke knocked him on his keister. When the Fireball got up Deke shucked his gloves and nailed that bastard in the chops. The Fireball went back down like a ton of bricks and then the shit hit the fan. Both benches got into it real good. It was a real nice scrap. We're banned from playing in the Gardens though. For life."

"Holy shit," Billy looked over at Deke, "You dropped the fuckin' Fireball?"

Before Deke could reply, the coach held up a hand.

"Awright! Awright! I've bin purty lenient with you guys. But I want you to cut out the goddamn language. Christ. You guys cuss like section hands. I want you to cut it out right now ... before you get me in trouble."

Billy grinned and gingerly clapped Deke on the back

"Well, thanks Pard. I guess me and the Fireball are even then?"

"Yeah," Deke replied. "He's really not a bad guy. I don't think he meant to bean you. I caught up with him just as he was leaning into the shot. It went higher than he thought it would. The bugger really has fast hands though. Before I knocked him down he got his own rebound and scored."

"Bill?" A voice came from the doorway. The Calder players turned their heads in unison and saw a clean-cut young man in suit and tie with a topcoat draped over his arm. He nervously twirled a pearl gray fedora in his hand as he stepped under one of the overhead lights, revealing a purple bruise on his cheek. He hesitated as the Calder players gathered protectively around Billy.

"Hey, fellas." The young man smiled disarmingly. "I just wanted to apologize to Bill and make sure he was O.K." He walked over to Billy and extended his hand. "Tommy Flynn. Sorry Bill, I can get a little aggressive in a game but I try to keep it clean. Sure didn't mean to raise it on you like that."

"Christ," Coach Zelenak said. "You got balls the size of church bells to come in here dressed like the fuckin' mayor of Edmonton." The coach made a move toward the young man but Deke stepped between them.

"It's O.K. " Billy said. Luck of the game I guess."

"Deke told me of a restaurant in the neighbour-

hood where I can buy you guys a soda or something. You in?"

"I'm in." Billy said.

Billy knew that Moira -- who had maintained a
relationship with his uncle since they met during
the war -- was Tommy's mother. Born in Britain,
Tommy had grown up to be a quintessential
Canadian boy, excelling at lacrosse, football and
hockey. When he attended Upper Canada College
in Ontario, he concentrated on hockey and began
to make a name for himself. He had a natural
talent for the game and, before long, teams like The
Toronto Maple Leafs and the Montreal Canadiens
began to express an interest in him.

After the game the boys met in a café in the
Cromdale area, near the arena. They were seated
in a booth with soft drinks in front of them, when
Tommy said: "Bill, I understand that you and I
have something in common."

"What would that be? I have a lump on my
noggin and you gave it me?"

"Well," Tommy grinned. "There's that too. But,
my mother has a gentlemen friend named Mingo
Perala, who I believe, is your uncle."

"That's right. Your mother is Moira. I met her
some years ago."

"Yes, the infamous Red Moira."

"I like her."

"She's a good sort." Tommy said. "She just
wasn't cut out to raise kids. My dad died in the war
and she's still pissed off about that. She handed me
over to live with my uncle when I was a baby so she

could spend all her time taking on the big munitions companies and warmongers of all sizes and shapes. But, I didn't come here to talk about my mother. You guys have a good team and I understand you have a good coach."

"We have two coaches," Billy said. "Mr. Zelenak and Ewan."

"Ewan Fraser?"

"Yep." Billy said."

"I've heard good things about him." Tommy said.

"Good things about who?" Deke asked, returning from the jukebox.

"Your dad. Ewan Fraser." Tommy said.

"He's not my dad. He's my uncle. My dad's brother." Deke had been aware of his relationship with Callum for some years. Tommy sat up, folded his elbows on the table, and moved forward in a conspiratorial manner.

"Deke, do you think I could become a paying guest in your house this winter? I'll pay whatever you want. It's just that I've heard so many good things about Ewan Fraser that I'd like to have him tutor me in hockey."

"Christ, you're the best bloody hockey player I've ever seen." Deke said, "You're a sure thing for the NHL. What more do you have to learn?"

"I want to improve my accuracy and my strength. I'm a little too light. I sometimes get bounced around pretty good."

Deke said: "I'd have to check with Ewan and

Faith but, they're both purty easy-going. I'll let you know."

"That would be great. Thanks Deke. I would like to start in October and stay until March."

On a sunny Sunday afternoon, in October of 1935, Deke, Billy, and the rest of the Calder boys, were gathered on the open field near the Fraser residence warming up for a pickup game of aerial football. A number of local girls had gathered by the baseball backstop, to watch the boys throw and kick a rugby ball around and were exchanging pleasantries when a large black Packard Twelve sedan rolled to a stop on the adjacent roadway. In depression-era Edmonton, especially in working class Calder, new Packards were as scarce as job openings and they elicited a great degree of awe and attention when they deigned to appear on local streets. Billy had seen the car before, having ridden in it when Moira had taken him for a haircut, bath and a new wardrobe in Dunblane.

Almost everyone in the vicinity of the field gravitated toward the elegant machine as the driver's door opened and Tommy Flynn, clad in tennis whites, stepped out. He called out to Deke and gestured to the Fraser house.

"I say, my good man, do you suppose that you and your chaps could carry my luggage into yonder house?"

Deke walked to the car, gave it several moments of scrutiny and said: "I don't see a piano tied to your ass, Mr. John Jacob Asshole. If you want that stuff in the house, you'll have to hump it yourself."

A giggle emanated from the partially open passenger side window, causing Deke to interrupt his discourse and peer in through the opening. A pretty young woman in tennis attire occupied the passenger seat and Deke -- mortified that his vulgar language had reached such ears -- blushed and mumbled an apology.

The girl, introduced as Tommy's cousin Dulci Flynn, had come along to drop Tommy and his effects at the Fraser house and then return the Packard to the downtown rail yard for shipment to Montreal. Dulci, Tommy and a number of Flynn relatives had spent the summer on the west coast and Moira had loaned them her Packard for transportation. Dulci was booked into the Macdonald Hotel for the night and entraining for her home in Montreal the following morning.

She exited the car, greeting Deke and Billy like long lost friends. With a tan, enhanced by her white tennis dress, Dulci dazzled the boys at the field. Billy cast an uncomfortable glance at Rena Pawluk -- a girl with whom he was friendly -- and felt a pang of regret as he saw her march to her bicycle and pedal away. He surmised that the appearance of the exotic Dulci Flynn had constituted a slap in the face to the Calder girls. Rena was a beautiful girl who could hold her own with any girls in blue jeans and school sweaters, but couldn't compete with the fashionable attire of the newcomer. Even her dress clothes, reserved for special occasions, couldn't match Dulci's elegance.

"Well, if no one is going to haul my luggage into

the house -- out of the goodness of their tiny little Edmonton hearts -- I'll just have to hire someone to do it." Tommy glanced at Mitch Pawluk, who was ogling Dulci. Mitch was fourteen at the time but he was a big boy and could hold his own on a football field or a hockey rink with guys that were four and five years his senior.

"Hi there Pal," Tommy offered a hand to Mitch. "I'm Tommy Flynn."

"Mitch Pawluk," Mitch said, shaking Tommy's hand. "I played against you last winter." Tommy clapped him on the back and said: "Wasn't that a game though?" He pulled a wad of bills from his pocket and plucked out a deuce.

"Would you like to drive this car over to the house and unload my luggage for a few bucks?"

Mitch's eyes lit up at the prospect of driving the car and at the sight of the money. Two dollars had a lot of buying power in the middle of the Great Depression and within minutes he was behind the wheel of the car, trying to orient himself to the controls.

"Dulci, why don't you help Mitch out with the car?"

"Normally, I wouldn't," Dulci smiled. "But, because he's so cute I will make an exception."

Dulci sat in the passenger beside Mitch, whose face was a bright shade of pink. She closed her door and, within minutes, the big car lurched into motion and made its way toward the house.

The remaining boys stood in awe at Mitch's good fortune with the money and the girl. To most of the boy's in the group, a quarter was a small fortune. A two-dollar bill was something approaching prosperity. Billy never wanted for 'walking around money' as he had a monthly stipend from his trust fund, established upon the sale of his Dunblane property. Deke had an allowance, mandated by Malcolm before he left the country. They were the only boys who hadn't expressed an interest in working for Tommy's cash.

When the Packard made its way back to the field, with Mitch at the wheel, Dulci rolled down her window and waved. "Hey Tommy," she said. "Mitch tells me that these boys were preparing to play a mean game of rugby. Think you can keep up with them?"

"Oh. I'm sure I can." Turning to Deke he said: What's say we choose sides and have a game of football?"

Deke walked up to Tommy, fingered a sleeve of his shirt and said: "Sure. But you are ya gonna play in that milkman outfit?"

Tommy's white pants, white shoes, and a white v-neck sweater seemed to glow in the early afternoon sun. Had it not been for his tanned complexion, he would have appeared ghostly, as his hair was a sun-bleached blonde.

"Why not?" Tommy says. "Nobody is going to catch me."

His statement was greeted by groans and catcalls from the boys on the field and from the growing group of bystanders who had been attracted to the field by the presence of the Packard.

Deke laughed. "Suit yourself. But when this game is over, they'll be calling you The Green Man. Remember ...you're not on the ice now, Mr. Fireball."

Deke and Tommy began picking sides. A coin flip gave Deke first choice. He picked Billy. Tommy picked Mitch Pawluk. Deke went on to pick Helmer Lindquist, Mitch Mitchell, Bobby Bahniuk, Ranny MacDonald and six younger kids. Tommy picked Ihor and Zenon Kovik, Johnny Arvine, Dusty Midbo, and six of the younger guys.

Aerial rugby was a hybrid game, which allowed for an indeterminate number of players to spend hours in pursuit of a football. A coin toss determined who kicked and who received.

At the kickoff, the receiving team would try to advance the ball as far as possible and then establish a line of scrimmage at the point where their ball carrier had been stopped. The quarterback would then line up behind the centre, who anchored a line that contained however many players on the team.

Tommy took the first snap but, before he could throw the ball, Deke charged through the line and flattened him. Tommy's white pants had suffered grass stains on the rear and both knees and his face was flushed as he came out of the huddle for second down. He took the snap, but this time his teammates formed a flying wedge and punched a hole in the opposing line. Tommy surged forward, flattened Deke and ran uncontested over the goal line. Tommy, obviously someone who loved to win, whooped and cavorted around the end zone. As there were no goal posts, converts were not a factor so the score stood at five-nothing.

Tommy kicked the ball directly at Deke who caught it and called for a block. Billy blocked Tommy by tackling him to the ground. Tommy yelled that he was being illegally held, but by that time Deke had run for a touchdown. Five-all.

The game settled down after that. Participants slugged it out for over an hour and signs of conflict manifested themselves in bloody noses, swollen lips and grass-stained clothing. Billy looked to the sidelines at one point and was surprised at the number of spectators who had assembled on the sidelines.

The game stalled at fifteen all and neither team seemed to be able to muster more points to win the game. Deke addressed his team in the huddle. "I don't know about you guys," Deke addressed his team in the huddle, "but I'm sick of this bloody game. What's say we just win it?"

Everyone agreed and Deke yelled to Tommy that the next points would win. Tommy agreed. Deke's team broke the huddle and lined up. Tommy's team was dug in on their side of the line with Tommy running back and forth behind them yelling, "Get the ball back -- make 'em fumble!"

Deke had devised a sleeper play that saw Billy drift to the sidelines while the rest of team blocked. When the ball was snapped Billy took off for the end zone. The remainder of the team gave Deke enough time to unlimber a pass that hit Billy in the end zone. While Deke's team celebrated the win, Tommy was apoplectic.

"That play was offside. No touchdown, Bill was over the line when the ball was snapped."

Tommy hated to lose but even his teammates, happy to pack it in, agreed that it was a touchdown. Dulci raised her voice, "Oh c'mon Tommy. Quit being a sore loser. You can't win them all. Sodas and hamburgers are on you."

Tommy good-naturedly footed the bill for the participants of the football game who hadn't gone home for Sunday dinner. When it came time for Dulci to leave, he, Deke and Billy dropped her off at the Macdonald and then drove the Packard to the freight sheds for transport. Then Tommy engaged a taxi to take them back to the Fraser house.

When the boys returned to the Fraser house that evening they heard the sounds of music emanating from Faith's gramophone in the parlour.

"Hey," Deke said. "Faith must be back from the lake. C'mon and meet her."

Tommy followed his new friends into the parlour and stopped in his tracks at the sight of the beautiful woman who sat on a sofa sorting through records.

Chapter 10

Rumours of War- 1939

EARLY IN 1939 MINGO RECEIVED A letter from Lylli
Koivisto -- whose family had remained in Karelia
after most North Americans had given up on the
experiment -- advising him that Toivo, had gone
missing after entering Karelia on a mission to
rescue her from her hard-line father.

Lylli had waited for him at a designated
location but he never arrived and soon afterward,
she discovered that Commissar Kosmynko was
holding him for ransom. The Commisar and his
cadre wanted $5,000 American dollars for Toivo.

Mingo raised the money but, a week before his
departure; one of his horses crushed him against
a corral stanchion breaking his right leg. Billy,
who lived and worked in Red Deer, volunteered to
deliver his brother's ransom and Mingo reluctantly
agreed to the arrangement.

After Billy arrived at the Edmonton bus

terminal, he went to a pre-arranged meeting with his uncle at the Lincoln Hotel beer parlour. Four empty glasses on the table bore witness to the fact that Mingo had fortified himself before meeting his nephew. Billy pulled a chair to the small round table and sat down across from his uncle.

"Hey Mingo. What's new?"

Mingo hunched over the small round table with his forearms on its terrycloth surface. He motioned for his nephew to sit down and signaled to the waiter for another round. A barman appeared with four glasses of beer on a tray. He looked at Billy and said: "How old are you son?" Twenty-one was the legal age in the province of Alberta at the time and Billy, at twenty, was one year short.

Before Billy could reply, Mingo said: "He's old enough Chuck. I'll vouch for him. Mingo's word carried weight in that particular bar, because he held an ownership position in the hotel.

"Whatever you say Mingo." The waiter put down the beer and retreated to the back of the almost empty barroom.

"Well Billy. I just thought that you and me should sit down and have a few beers before you ship out. It might be awhile before we see each other again and I just wanted ...to start out by tellin' ya ..." Mingo took a pull from his glass, "I shoulda spent more time with you while you were growin' up."

"Jesus!" Billy laughed. "What do you mean -- did I turn out bad or something?"

"No, no, no. Christ... you turned out to be a real

good man. I'm proud to be your uncle. I just never took the time to tell you. You know...that I care about ya."

"Jeez." Billy said uneasily. "That's O.K. I know you do. Hell, you've looked after me since I was little kid. You sure don't have to apologize for that."

"I think I do Bill. It was my duty to feed and put clothes on yer back, but I never told you how I felt about ya. When I took you out of Dunblane -- all those years ago -- I thought you'd be a pain in the ass, what with being spoiled by Anya and all. But, you bin a good soldier. You never complained about your lot in life, or the times I wasn't there when you needed me. And I never told you." He paused for another sip.

"Never told me what?"

Mingo cleared his throat, took a long pull of his beer, and then setting the glass on the table, raised his eyes and said.

"I've never told ya...you know... that I cared fer ya. Yer like my own son but I never told ya that. I guess I was just bein' chickenshit about it. Moira and Faith are always on me to let you know how I feel about you. I just kept puttin' it off. Now, with you goin' to the old country, I can't put it off no more."

"Aw, that's O.K.," Billy waved dismissively. "I know you care about me. Hell, I haven't always been the easiest guy to get along with either."

"Now that," Mingo slapped his knee and grinned at his nephew, "is just a load of fresh, steamin' bullshit!"

"No, it's not." Billy insisted. "I've done some stupid things."

Mingo reached over and squeezed his nephew's shoulder.   "Believe me, young Billy Jurva... your sins don't amount to a hill o' beans. Far's I know, you've never let anybody down and you've always been a straight shooter. I'm really sorry to see you go, but I think Toivo's in a bad spot an' he needs our help. Trouble is ... things are really getting hot over there and I want you to know what to expect. You have enough money to pay the ransom and grease some palms. When you find Toivo, try to get him the hell into Norway. From there, catch a ship to Scotland. If you are unlucky enough to get drafted -- because of yer Finn name -- try to get yourself into a rear echelon job. A pencil pusher behind the lines, something like that."

"Geez, Mingo, I'm not going to chicken out."

"I know, I know. But, just humour me for a minute. Sit back and let me have my say. Take it from someone who knows. You do not want to go into combat cuz it'll screw you up fer life."

"Can it that bad."

"It sure as hell can. In 1916 at the Somme one of my buddies was standing beside me when we were getting ready to over the top. A German shell came in and ... my friend..." Mingo was silent for several moments, "Well... he just disintegrated. In a second he became a mist of blood, brains and shit that covered one side of me, from head to toe. I spent that day in No-Man's-Land covered with what was left of my friend. He was spread over me like a coat of paint. I remember praying that old Fritzie would put me out of my misery that day."

"Jee-sus!" Billy breathed. "Wouldn't they let you stay behind and get cleaned off?"

"There was no time for that. We had three of four yards of mud to take."

"Christ, that's terrible..."

"Yeah. It is. You see Bill ... soldiers don't die clean, like in the movies. They don't just grab their chest and slowly collapse with a little string a' blood running from the corner of their mouth. No... what really happens is; they get buried alive ... they drown in mud ... they disintegrate ... they get their heads blown off ... they lose arms and legs. They end up lying in a shell hole tryin' to stop their guts from sliding out of their body, while watching big fat trench rats fight to see who gets the first taste.

When you walked in No-Man's-Land, you walked on a carpet of corpses, some old some new; body parts of all descriptions, dead men, dead horses and a lot of unexploded ordnance. You pissed or shat yourself sometimes because your body just ain't designed for the shock of frontline combat.

Consider yourself lucky that I don't have the words to describe the smell and the foul water that we stood in; a mixture of blood, dirt, shit, piss, and rotting bodies that pulled you in like quicksand. Some guys just sank out of sight and were never seen again.

The parapets were the garbage dumps of the

trenches. Everything, including corpses, was strewn on the lip of the trenches so you had to crawl through it when you went over the top. Sometimes a guy would buy it while leaving the trench and his body would add to the rotting pile."

"How could you keep from going crazy?" Billy said.

"Every once in a while some poor sweat would lose his mind and run for it. They'd catch him and he'd get a drumhead court martial and a firing squad at dawn. It didn't matter how brave you had been. If you snapped and left your post, or just dozed off, you could be shot at sunrise. That's why I always respected the Aussies. They never bought into that shit."

"My God, how could you fight for such bastards? Why didn't you mutiny like those French soldiers you once told me about?"

"First of all, we didn't fight for those bastards, we fought for each other. We didn't fight for Canada, the King, or because Kaiser Bill had to be stopped. We fought for each other! You supported the men in your platoon because they did the same for you. Oh sure, we had pride in ourselves. We realized, sometime after the Somme, that we were the best troops around. But, that made it all the worse when a butcher like Haig sent such good soldiers into the teeth of machine gun fire. The boys were cut down in windrows but they kept sending us over the top."

"Jee-sus," Billy breathed. I had no idea."

"There was no reason you would know about

it. The newspaper writers, politicians and those bastards in the recruiting offices; the limp pricks, who have never heard a bullet fired in anger, would never tell you the real story. Their job is to paint a rosy picture of King, Country, Duty, and Courage. Last war they had women on the streets handing out white feathers to any man who they thought should be in uniform. They had it all figured out. If you wouldn't enlist on your own they'd shame you into it. Archie Bzeta, who was shot up at Passchendaele and had a road map of scars on his body, was walking down Stephen Avenue in Calgary in civvies when one a' those self-righteous bitches walked up and gave him a white feather. He gave her a shove and all hell broke loose. A bunch of civilians jumped him and ended up breaking one of his arms.

Remember this Bill. To the guvamint, dead heroes are better than live ones. The live ones can be embarrassing; they show up in public with missing arms and legs, get drunk and disorderly, or just sit on the street in their wheelchairs and remind civilians of what the people in power actually think of rank-and-file citizens. We were all just numbers to the bloodthirsty bastards who threw us against bob-wire and machine guns. They knew we'd never make it but they were honour-bound to answer Fritzie 'cause he did the same thing the day before. You know that Haig considered 75% casualties 'manageable?'"

"I've never heard you talk like this before." Billy said.

"I don't talk about what happened over there. It is impossible to tell anyone -- who wasn't there -- what it was like."

"Did you talk about it with Ewan...he was there."

"Ewan sure as hell doesn't want to talk about it. After serving in the trenches, he spent some time pulling mangled men and horses out of bombed out trains. When the Black Crows show up he finds himself a bottle of whiskey and runs for the hills."

"Black Crows?"

"That's what we call the bad memories that catch up with us once in awhile."

"So, when the Black Crows show up, you saddle up old Spud and jump fences, or ski for miles in the winter."

"Yes, that and Moira. Without Moira, Faith and you, I may not have made it. You guys helped me shake off the bad days."

"Me too?"

"Yep. Ever since you showed up, you made a difference. All of you gave me something to think about besides my time in France. Some of the guys killed themselves after they came home because they were afraid to go to sleep at night and suffer the nightmares. I try to put them behind me but they boil up from time to time. When I wake up from a nightmare I curse those bastards in the High Command and relegate them to the deepest reaches of Hell for what they did to us.

As bad as we had it, some other troops had it worse. French troops finally mutinied after being slaughtered in battle after battle. The poor bloody Russians were treated like dogs and the Brits just kept marching into hell. Singing *God Save the King.*"

"What about the Yanks?"

"Who? The famous Rainbow Division -- the ones who came out after the storm was over? They thought they just had to show up and say 'boo,' and Fritzie would run away screaming. Nah, they weren't players in spite of all their bullshit. They convinced anybody, who'd listen, that they won the war. But they didn't do anything near what the rest a' us did. A guy I know, who spent four years in France with the Machine Gun Corps, once put one a' those bigmouths in his place. This guy, Dick Berrington, was in a coffee shop somewhere near the border when this Yank comes in and starts braggin' about how they won the war. Dick sits there quietly until he's heard enough. He stands up, slams his hand on the counter and says: "You want to know who won that war? The Canadians and Lloyd-George. That's who won the bloody war!"'

The Yank buttoned his lip -- after doing what they usually always do -- apologize all over the place about not meaning to hurt anybody's feelings and offering to buy everybody a coffee. Nobody took him up on it. Dick's coffee was on the house though.

Fer years I've had this daydream. All the Old Sweats on our side of the line, and all the Fritzie footsloggers from across the wire, would declare a truce. When all those staff officers -- the ones who sent us over the top every day -- showed up to see what the hell was going on, they would be forced to fight the German staff. Then, the rest of us, footsloggers on both sides of the line, would down weapons and watch the show.

They wouldn't be allowed to use weapons. Just bare hands. When the rest of us got tired of watching them squeal and holler; we would march them into the mud of Passhendaele until their snouts went under and they drowned in the mud. Then, all of us would go home."

Part 3

Chapter 11- The Winter War

Finland - 1939

BILLY'S LEG MUSCLES PULSED IN AGONY as he made the final strides to gain the summit of the hill above the frozen lake. The Russian 163rd Division was bivouacked on the lake ice en route to Suomussalmi where Finnish intelligence reported that they intended to link up with their 44th Division and effectively cut Finland into two sections.

A wave of relief washed over him as he reached the top and relaxed to let his skis carry him down the slope. The Finnish ski troops had traveled for over 20 hours in a wide flanking movement to engage the Russians. On the trail below him, Billy could see the leaders of his column move onto lake ice to initiate the attack. As he swept toward the shore, Billy looped the straps of his ski poles over his wrists and pulled the Suomi submachine gun -- that had hung at his back -- around to rest against his chest. Pulling back the charging handle he gripped the weapon in both hands and joined a second wave of attackers now forming a skirmish line along the shore.

An irregular line of white-clad figures moved across the ice toward the Russian position. The first wave had engaged the enemy and -- as he approached the killing ground -- Billy heard the sounds of rifle fire and the distinctive rattle of the Suomis. There were also sounds of explosions and return fire and he became aware of the sounds of men screaming. The condition of the disorganized, dead and dying Russians, ill equipped for the winter conditions, bothered him but he steeled himself for the job at hand by evoking memories of his father's fate at the hands of the Soviets.

The Russians were rolling on the snow and fleeing the fires that had given them comfort from the frigid Finnish night. The dark-clad enemy stood out in contrast to the snow and offered easy targets for the Finns. As Billy lifted his Suomi and sprayed a hail of bullets into a group of men who were attempting to set up a machine gun, a loud explosion on his left almost rocked him off of his skis but he continued firing until he exhausted the magazine.

Replacing the spent magazine with a full one, Billy continued firing at the enemy assuming that they must be screaming or shouting, especially the ones writhing in the snow, but he heard nothing.

He saw the muzzle flashes from his weapon but didn't hear the sounds of gunfire.

A Russian with his lower jaw shot away lurched into Billy's path and he dispatched him with a burst from the Suomi. Another reeled drunkenly, gripping his throat with both hands as he attempted to staunch a gush of blood from his severed jugular. Billy swiveled his weapon and pressed the trigger. The man's head exploded and his body reeled awkwardly for several seconds before folding to the ground.

Some Russian transport had been fired and the flaming vehicles provided a surreal backdrop to the tableau on the ice. The first attack had severed the Russian convoy and the ski troops established a perimeter in the opening, forcing the Russians to split up and retreat. The segments of the sundered convoy were forced into areas where other Finnish ground forces awaited them. The ski troops dug in and held their positions until an infantry regiment arrived to relieve them several hours after the initial attack.

The Russians had invaded Finland in 1939 with visions of an easy victory. They brought parade bands to herald their victory but no supplies for a long campaign. Their soldiers, in dark unseasonal uniforms, were sitting ducks for the white-clad Finns and, without adequate clothing for the Arctic environment, the Russians spent much of their time huddled around fires.

"The fish will be fat this spring ... all of our lakes will be full of dead Russians," Sergeant Kako,

Billy's platoon leader, had remarked after the ski troops had regrouped in a wooded area several miles from the attack site.

After the bivouac site was established, Billy broke out his rations and waited for his brother to arrive. Through an underground group, he had ransomed his brother from Soviet custody in Karelia. Upon receipt of the ransom money, Commissar Kosmynko had released Toivo into Billy's custody.

Toivo had no intention of escaping to Norway, his animus towards the Soviets had only been increased by his incarceration and, his first move was to link up with his militia unit and begin training for the inevitable invasion. He had counseled his brother to return to Canada but Billy was caught up in exploring the homeland of his ancestors and spending time with the beautiful Finnish girls who considered him an exotic creature from the New World.

Billy dallied too long. On November 30th 1939, the Soviets invaded Finland. Toivo had Billy inducted into his unit of ski troops so he could keep an eye on his kid brother and have a hand in his training. It became their ritual to eat together whenever on operations, and after the bivouac had been established, Billy waited at the agreed-upon location. Toivo, a captain who had led his company in the first attacking wave, was uncharacteristically late so Billy packed his rations back into his haversack and set off to find him.

Billy found Toivo's platoon busy setting up a

perimeter at the rear of the encamped Finns. They were entrenched in the snow and ice and positioned to alert the main body against a possible Russian counter attack. Billy spotted his brother among a group of soldiers and made his way towards him. Toivo broke away from a group of white-clad soldiers, spotted Billy and waved as he strode across the snow towards him.

The sound of clanking tank treads electrified the ski troops and, as Toivo turned back to his men, Billy saw a Soviet T-26 Voroshilov tank emerge from under the limbs of snow-covered fir trees. He dropped to his stomach and aimed his Suomi at the oncoming vehicle. As he lined his sights on the turret, he saw a number of men converge on either side of the machine. The men were carrying tree trunks, which they jammed into the tank's drive sprockets, bringing the machine to a halt. Another wave of attackers appeared wielding Molotov cocktails and incendiary bombs, which were thrown under the belly of the T-26. The two-man crew was 'smoked' out of their vehicle and emerged onto the hull with hands raised.

The brothers were less than ten metres apart when the sound of aircraft heralded a Russian bombing run. Toivo signaled to his brother to hit the ground then turned and disappeared into a red mist. Billy attempted to reach his brother but a wall of snow erupted in front of him and he felt the ground buckle under his feet. He felt himself propelled into the air where his body made a slow rotation before returning to the icy surface.

Chapter 12

Ortona Italy - 1943

IN 1939, AT THE OUTSET OF the war, the Calder boys were in their late teens and early twenties. Most of them worked on the railway. Deke was a brakeman on freight service; Mitch, Ihor and Zenon were switchmen. Peewee was a car checker. Johnny Arvine and Dusty Midbo were 'car knockers' whose job was to inspect each wheel on a departing train, and with the tap of their long handled hammer, listen for any irregularity in the steel wheel.

On advice from Moira, Billy had invested in a small oilfield service company in Turner Valley and began learning the business by spending time at well sites. He had gone to Finland, to get his brother out of Soviet custody in Karelia and hadn't been heard from since. Tommy was playing hockey in the Maple Leafs' system somewhere in Ontario.

Ewan, who had served with the Canadian Corps of Railway Troops during the previous war, had been offered the rank of captain and promptly departed for Europe as an officer on loan to the British Army.

Mingo and Moira were in Portugal helping to relocate refugees from the recently ended Spanish Civil War. They helped repatriate wounded veterans of the Mackenzie Papineau battalion -- who had fought as a Canadian unit during that war -- but were considered outlaws by the Canadian government and often denied reentry. Faith and Rosie were the sole occupants of the Fraser home.

One Friday night in February of 1940, Peewee, his face flushed, entered the Calder Café and joined Deke, Ihor, Johnny and Mitch, who were sitting on stools at the counter. Although Peewee was now one of the taller members of the group, he hadn't been able to shed his childhood nickname.

"That new afternoon yardmaster is a real asshole." He said.

A waitress cautioned him about his language and his face reddened and he looked down and muttered "Sorry."

"What happened now?" Ihor said.

"The sonofabitch tagged me with two brownies." The waitress said: "William," and Peewee scowled and hunched his shoulders.

"Two demerits? That's bugger-all," said Johnny. "What'd you do... piss on his shoes?" The waitress approached and stood with hands on hips.

"If you boys can't watch your language, you'll have to leave."

"No," Peewee continued. "I let a car with arch bar trucks go out on a 403."

"Peewee." Johnny said. "That's a speed train. Those old arch bars can crack like that," he snapped his fingers, "and put a train on the ground."

"Well, thanks for backing me up, Mr. Company Man."

"I don't know why I listen to your bitching anyway," Johnny said. "What you plannin' to do about it?"

"I'll tell you what I've done about it." Peewee said. "I quit my job. Tomorrow...I'm goin' to join up."

The boys were silent for several moments. Then Deke spoke. "When you goin'?'

"I'm goin' to th' Armoury first thing in the morning."

"Give it a couple a' days and I'll go with ya." Deke said.

"If yer goin' then I'm goin' too." Ihor slapped the table with an open palm. "I'm bettin' that Zenon will come with us." The waitress stood and stared. "You crazy boys," she said, shaking her head as she collected empty soft drink bottles from the boys. "You don't know what you're getting yourselves into."

So it was decided. Deke, Peewee, Ihor, and Mitch enlisted in the Eddies (the 49th Edmonton Regiment) on the following Monday. To a man they were disappointed when they were not issued with uniforms and weapons and sent off to war at once. They were sent home and told to return in a week for medicals. During that week, Zenon Kovik decided to follow his brother and friends into the ranks. Johnny Arvine and Dusty Midbo also decided to take the King's shilling.

Given an unexpected week to say his goodbyes, Deke was able to visit his lady friends. He had never spent much time with girls his own age because he wasn't patient enough to win their affections to the point where he could bed them. He had discovered early on that most contemporary females of his acquaintance required a ring or a long-term commitment before they would give up what he was seeking. 'Wham bam' encounters were not satisfactory as he required time and space to fully enjoy the experience. Hurried hookups usually involved women who simply wanted to get it over with. As a result, his sexual experience was very limited until he took a summer job delivering invoices for the gas company. The long, hot, sweltering summer of 1936, when he delivered gas bills door to door -- often shirtless because of the temperature -- was one that he would never forget. On his first day, a thirtyish woman, who looked like Rita Hayworth, invited him into her house for cold lemonade. While he sat drinking the beverage, his hostess languidly disrobed in front of him before taking his hand and leading him into her bedroom. Over the course of that afternoon he learned how to make love to a woman; an ability that would stand him in good stead in the future. He spent the remainder of that summer in a state of ecstasy after he discovered that a lot of salesman, railroad firemen and brakemen had young wives who led boring lives when their husbands were on the road or in the Airport Hotel beer parlour talking 'railroad.' Armed with his new skill set, Deke made connections with a number of these restless women. And established, what his friend's enviously referred to as 'Deke's Trapline.'

Marjorie Wilson dropped her head back and sighed deeply as Deke disengaged and moved back off of the bed. Unclothed save for a pair of panties, encircling one ankle, she lay panting for several moments before pushing herself up to a sitting position against the headboard. Reaching for a package of Sweet Caporals on the bedside table, she waved the package at Deke who was pulling on his trousers.

"Smoke?"

He shook his head, "I gotta to get going. The Army gets really pissed off if yer late." Although the army hadn't yet monopolized all of his time, Deke used it as a convenient excuse to leave.

"You still screwing Bill Perchuk's wife?"

"What? Deke froze and gaped at her.

"Don't give me that innocent look I know yer porking her. Just a word to the wise, is all. Bill is getting' mighty suspicious about what Edna is up to when he's workin' midnights."

"How do you know that?" Deke said changing his mind about the cigarette.

"Well, Bill and I get together every so often -- if you catch my drift -- and alls I'm tellin' yuh," she said as she lit his cigarette with a table lighter, "is that you should just take Edna off a' yer trap line. Bill is not a guy you want to fool with."

"Shit. I can handle Perchuk."

"If you meet him face-to-face maybe. But, Perchuk will always come from behind you. Usually with a baseball bat or an ax handle."

"Yeah? Well, screw Perchuk and his little red wagon. What about your husband?" Deke exhaled a cloud of smoke. "Did he figure out what you do in yer spare time?"

"Wilf? That's a good one. Since they made him a yardmaster he's bin banging a blonde bimbo who works in the Divisional Superintendent's office. Hey, I'm leaking. Get me one a' them tissues from the dresser willya sweetie?"

Deke pulled several tissues from a box and walked back to the bed. She opened her thighs and he pushed the soft paper up into her to stem the flow. Wiping away an escaping stream from her upper thighs with his hand, he smeared it on her breasts."

"S'posed to be good for your skin." He said.

"You're good for my skin. When am I gonna see you again?"

"When that asshole Hitler is hangin' by his balls in the Prince of Wales Armoury."

"Well, take yer time goin' there. But hurry back." She smiled as she watched the muscular young man pull a shirt over his head.

"Hey, yer fly is open." She laughed. "Don't want Deke Junior catchin' cold, now do we?"

She giggled and waved as he left the room.

None of the Calder boys washed out as a result of their physicals and were soon installed in pre-fabricated huts behind the Prince of Wales Armoury. While they waited for equipment and clothing, they were lectured by regular army NCOs in military routine, regimental history and poison gas training and, when nothing else was on the schedule, they were sent on numerous route marches. In September they were issued with uniforms and in October, rifles. Looking in the mirror they now felt like real soldiers.

The Eddies learned that they were to be an element of the Second Brigade of the Canadian First Division, The Old Red Patch, and they learned that they would serve beside the Seaforth Highlanders from Vancouver and an iconic regular force regiment, Princess Patricia's Canadian Light Infantry.

The First Division, with no appropriate winter quarters in Canada, had been ordered to Britain in December. Edmontonians in the unit were all granted three-day passes and the Calder boys looked forward to a party at the Fraser house on their first night.

Since he had hired on with the railway, Deke had lived in a small suite near the rail yard and rarely visited Faith, after Ewan went overseas, because his lack of seniority deemed that he work long hours on the road in the way freight service and because he felt he had an unnatural interest in the woman who had raised him.

After spending time with their families, the

newly minted soldiers began showing up at the Fraser house in the early evening. They were all in uniform, complete with blancoed web belts and gaiters and boots with mirror-like finishes.

Johnny Arvine and Rena Pawluk energetically jitterbugged to music emanating from a floor-model gramophone while a number of people cheered and clapped in encouragement. In addition to the dancers, soldiers and civilians sat or stood around the large parlour.

When it appeared that all of the boys were present, Faith stood and announced. "We have a surprise for our soldier boys. A special guest just blew in from Ontario. She gestured to the kitchen doorway and a grinning Tommy Flynn emerged. The boys fell upon him, good naturedly roughing him up, pounding him on the back and pumping his hand.

Tommy was in civvies, prompting Deke to say: "Hey Flynn, you sitting out this war?"

"Noop. I didn't want you guys to hog all the glory so I enlisted today. Soon as I got off the train."

"We're shipping out on Friday. You coming with us?" Deke said.

"I hope so. Say...where's Jurva?"

"He went to Finland to link up with his long lost brother." Peewee said. "He'll probably be sitting out the war bare naked in a sauna with a couple a' them good looking Finn girls."

When asked of Billy's whereabouts, Faith and Mingo had remained close-mouthed about what they knew of his fate. They knew of Toivo's death but Billy's state of health and whereabouts were unknown.

Tommy spotted Mingo. He was seated at the dining room table playing cards with an attractive woman in a Medical Corps uniform. The woman's uniform had lieutenant's pips on each shoulder.

"Moira sends her regards and expects you in Montreal for New Year's Eve."

"I'll be there." Mingo smiled at his defacto son and, noticing that Tommy was looking questioningly at his companion, said: "Tommy Flynn, meet Lieutenant Dara McKnight. She's shipping out on Friday with the First Div."

"Rosie has told me all about you." Dara smiled. "You're the famous hockey player."

"Tommy." Faith waved at him from the gramophone. "Put on some of those records that you brought."

"Isn't she breathtaking?" Dara said, nodding at Faith. "They don't make women like her anymore. Get over there and play her some music."

Tommy moved to the gramophone, slid a record from its paper sleeve, placed it on the turntable and when the music began, held out a hand. All eyes were on Faith as Tommy led her to the middle of the floor. Her shapely body telegraphed itself through the soft material of her dress as she moved to the music. Her chestnut hair, cut in a pageboy style, bounced around her face as she moved to the music sang along with the lyrics. A tendril curled down over her forehead accenting her large, wide set green eyes. When she smiled, which was often, her features cooperated to give her face a radiant glow.

The couple danced to beat of an energetic swing tune, eliciting shouts of praise from the spectators. When the record ended Tommy bowed to Faith and thanked her for the dance. Then he turned to the gramophone, lifted the pickup arm from the recording, removed the black disk from the turntable and replaced it with another. When the strains of a waltz began to emanate from the speaker, Tommy walked over to a smiling young girl and pulled her onto the floor.

"Let's cut a rug Rosie."

Rosie beamed with pleasure as Tommy led her to the centre of the floor while Faith turned and approached Peewee.

"C'mon soldier boy, let's see what you can do." Peewee's face reddened and he looked so panicstricken that Faith smiled and patted his cheek. Deke stood up as she surveyed the room for a partner but Faith ignored him and crooked a finger at Johnny Arvine, who was known to be a good dancer.

"C'mon Johnny, let's show the folks how it's done."

Johnny grinned and led her to an open area on the hardwood floor. Deke felt awkward as he stood and watched Johnny conduct her around the floor. He felt a surge of envy as Johnny's hand curved around her slim waist and he left the room, removing his cigarette case from a breast pocket of his tunic. As he patted himself for matches, a light appeared in front of him.

"Light?" A woman's voice asked.

"Thanks." Deke said, sucking the flame into his cigarette.

"When she raised her lighter and lit her own cigarette, he asked: "Do I know you?"

"You might say that we are acquainted."

"And how might you say we are acquainted?" Deke smiled.

"Well, do you remember a skeletal creature who used to live in your attic?"

Deke held out his hand for her lighter, ignited it and illuminated her face.

"You. Her...No! You can't be the same..." Deke's jaw dropped and he shook his head as he returned her lighter.

"I would never have recognized you. So, now you're in the army?"

"Yes I'm back on the up and up."

"But how did someone like you ever end up at Ozzies?"

"It's a long story. So, I'll give you the short version. My people are wealthy brewery owners in Montreal. They had me lined up to marry a boring lawyer and become a boring housewife but I wanted to study medicine. My father didn't think that was the kind of work a woman should do; he thought I should settle down and begin producing his grandsons. You see I was an only child and, after I was born, my mother became barren. They blamed her condition on me and applied a lot of pressure on me to forego my medical studies and settle down.

"Barren?"

"She couldn't have any more babies."

"Oh."

"When I refused to comply with their wishes, they refused to pay for my university education. If it hadn't have been for a sympathetic grandmother, I wouldn't have made it, but I finally got my degree. As an intern I was given a backbreaking schedule and all the shit jobs. A fellow intern offered me some drugs that would help me stay awake but I refused to use them. I often found myself falling asleep on the job and was given several warnings and, finally, an ultimatum. One more instance of sleeping on the job would result in dismissal so I gave in. My friend provided the drugs and I never fell asleep on duty again. I used the drugs in order to prove that I could take anything they could hand out but, when they discovered that I had a habit, I was fired."

"Aw shit. Uh...pardon my French."

"You're pardoned. Anyway...I landed a job at the Royal Alex in Edmonton, through the influence of an uncle. The pace was slower and I was able to wean myself from drugs over several months. I was doing well until..."

"Until what?" Deke said, now caught up in the story.

"Until my former associate showed up. His drug use led to his dismissal in Montreal and he followed me to Edmonton."

"That wasn't good."

"Actually... I was happy to see him. I was so lonely out here. I didn't know anyone and I was living under a microscope because the Chief of Staff knew of my previous problems. To make a long story short, my friend and I began to burn the candle at both ends and one night, after attending several parties in the city, we ended up at Ozzies. I passed out. When I woke up, Ozzie told me that I was his property. It turned out that my companion got himself into a high stakes poker game and ended up losing me to Ozzie."

"But... that's against the law. He couldn't do that." Deke said.

"Well, he did. Law not withstanding. White Slavery exists here in Alberta, as it does almost everywhere. Ozzie showed me a contract, which showed that my noble companion 'sold' me into the flesh trade."

"Couldn't you have just busted out?"

"No. I became Ozzie's prize whore. When I wasn't working, I was locked in a room. It was Chance's job to keep an eye on me. Ozzie told Chance that he would have his nuts if I ever escaped. When Ozzie wasn't around, Chance would take me into his room to get his share."

Deke shook his head and gave his smoke a long pull. "Those goddamn Callanders. I knew Ozzie was a bad son of a bitch. I just didn't think he was that bad. "

"Believe me. He was that bad. I was so happy when I heard that Rosie had escaped. She didn't know of my existence at the Compound, but I often looked through a keyhole during the day and was aware of her existence. I was worried what would happen to her when she matured."

"Y'know? If that son-of-a-bitch wasn't dead... I'd kill him." Deke said, stubbing out his cigarette and shaking another from its pack.

"Ozzie is dead?" Dara said as she lit Deke's cigarette

"Yeah. Last year. A trapper from Lac La Biche, gutted him with a hunting knife."

"Omigod."

"Ozzie tried to boot the guy out of a whore's room...uh, I'm sorry I..."

"No apology required. I'm not a whore any more. Thanks to Faith Fraser."

"Well," Deke continued. "The trapper didn't agree that his time was up so, when Ozzie came in wavin' a shotgun, he countered with his skinning knife."

"Well, I can't say that I'm too broken up about Ozzie's demise. There were rumors that Ozzie and Chance had done a girl in and I was terrified of them. I know that one of girls from Saskatchewan disappeared and was never seen again."

"What happened to your boyfriend? The one who sold you to Ozzie?"

"As far as I know, he disappeared into the States"

"But, Faith and Billy drove out there. To the Compound" You should a caught a ride out with them."

"I was so strung out that day. Ozzie just got some new heroin and he didn't trust the source so he used me as a guinea pig. I was out of my mind when they showed up. They tell me I staggered out of the Compound naked and confronted Faith."

"Yeah. You caused Billy to do a double take."

"I assume that he told all his cronies about me."

"You don't know Billy. He didn't tell anyone. You see, Faith asked him not to spread it around and, because he worships her, he never told anyone. It was that asshole Chance who spread the news."

"Well, thank God for Faith and Billy. I heard of how she backed Ozzie down when he came for me. How all of you saved me. Believe me, I am eternally grateful to all of you. What is the word on Billy?"

"We don't know where he is. We know he was wounded in Finland and his brother was killed. We haven't heard a word since."

"Oh, God I pray he's O.K." Dara said grasping Deke's arm.

"We're all hopin' for the best."

"It's terrible when it happens to someone like Billy, something like that should only happen to slugs like the Callanders. I suppose it would be too much to ask that Chance be dead too?"

Deke chuckled ruefully. "He's still alive. But, since Ozzie bought it, Chance has hit some hard times. With Ozzie gone, the law moved in and shut the Compound down. I hear he's running with a gang of idiots who think they're some kind of big time gangsters."

"Oh excuse me Derek. Here's my ride. I have to run in and say goodbye to Faith and Rosie."

Deke looked up to see an army Jeep pull into the yard. Dara called out to the driver:

"Hold on Corporal. I'll be there in a minute."

"Yes Ma'am." The driver responded.

When Dara returned to the house, Deke walked over to the Jeep.

"Well, Corp. How's it hanging?

"It's not hanging. It's strapped to my ankle."

"What's yer unit? Service Corps?"

"Yep." The driver offered his hand. Maurice Douville."

"Deke Fraser. You shipping out with the First Div.?"

"Nah, I'm on chauffeur duty here. I drive all a' the piss tank officers from party to party. You'd be shocked at the amount of tail those guys get."

"What about the looey yer drivin' now? I'd hate to think that you'd call her a piss tank."

The driver straightened in his seat, "Lieutenant McKnight? No way she's a piss tank. She don't drink. She don't party. She's a good sort. My sister's in her unit and those nurse's would cut out yer giblets and fry 'em up in onions, if they knew you said a bad word about her."

Deke grinned. 'Glad to hear that... she's a friend of the family."

"So," the corporal said, looking at Deke's shoulder flashes. The Eddies, eh? My old man used to talk about you guys. He was in the last war."

Dara rushed up to the Jeep. She stopped,

planted a kiss on Deke's cheek and got into the vehicle.

"See you." She waved. "Over there."

The second day of the three-day pass started in the beer parlour of the Airport Hotel on 127th Avenue. Although Tommy was the only one who was of legal age, the waiters looked the other way and served the rest of the boys. When the Air Force arrived in the person of LAC Johnny Rankin, and LAC Charlie Forrestell, plans were made to patronize the Palace Gardens, a dance hall on the east end of Jasper Avenue.

The boys in uniform were warmly welcomed by the crowd at the dance hall and a friendly atmosphere prevailed until shortly before midnight when the girl that Deke was dancing with suddenly announced: "Oh oh! Trouble coming in the door."

Deke turned to see a number of young men in bizarre, brightly coloured suits strut into the room. The suits featured wide-lapelled, big-shouldered jackets, which reached almost to their knees, trousers with a deep waistband festooned with mother of pearl buttons and wide knees that narrowed down to cuffs that hugged their ankles. They all wore wide-brimmed fedoras.

"What th' hell is all this?" Deke asked his partner.

"Zoot Sooters," the girl said. "I'm getting out of here."

"Stick around." Deke said.

"No, I'm leaving. See, they've already brushed by the bouncers."

"Kee-rist." Peewee said. They look like the gangsters in Li'l Abner."

"Yeah, they do. There's fifteen a' them. Seven of us."

"We might get help from some of the crowd." Peewee said.

"I wouldn't count on it." Deke said. "The bouncers might support us, but my thinking is... we're on our own. Go round up the others."

A bouncer approached Deke. "They've torn the receiver off of the phone, so we can't call the cops. If you guys are leaving, will you go the Police Station and tell them what's happening here?"

"We're not running from a bunch of cartoon weasels." Deke said. "Now, how do you want to play this?"

"Well," said the bouncer. "My job is to see that no paying customers get hurt. If you guys stand between the Zoots and the crowd and get them facing you, one a' my boys will run out the back door and go to the cops. The rest of us will hit them from behind."

The bouncer left as the Kovik brothers came up, each with an arm around the waist of a dance partner.

"Looks like the Circus is in town." Zenon said.

"They look like clowns," one of the girls said. "But, they carry sawed off pool cues and switchblades. And they like to beat up on soldiers"

The Zoots had formed a circle on the dance floor and were circulating a bottle of rye. When the bottle was empty it was thrown onto the dance floor with such force that it shattered. Then they all turned around slowly and began to scan the crowd.

Peewee returned with Johnny and Dusty and the two airmen.

"Holy shit." Peewee said. "One a' them is Chance Callander. Another one is Spitter Smatello."

"Hey Chance. Soldier boys." A voice, which Deke recognized as Spitter's, was heard above the buzz of the crowd.

"What say we find out how tough they are?"

Chance smirked as he made his way toward Deke, who stood with his friends around him.

"Well, well. If it ain't my old nemesis Deke Fraser."

"Wow." Deke said "Nemesis, eh? Someone teach you how to read?"

"You always were a smartass Fraser. But this time you ain't got yer knuckledusters. An' yer old lady ain't waving a rifle at me. This is what I got," he reached into a pants pocket and removed a sawed-off pool cue, which he held up to Deke, who said: "Put that thing away or I'll shove it so far up yer ass that it'll chip yer teeth. What's say you and me settle this outside? Just the two of us."

"Oh, so you can cold cock me with a knuckle-duster like you did the last time?

"I thought you said I didn't have a knuckleduster? Besides, I was just a kid when that happened. Eight years old. You were in yer teens. This time I won't need a knuckleduster."

"Hoo hoo." Chance turned to his followers, who

had massed behind him. He puts on a uniform on and he thinks he's a tough guy."

"I'm not a tough guy, but I'm tough enough to punch yer lights out."

"You know Fraser, I don't need a club." He handed the pool cue to Spitter and pulled a knife handle from a jacket pocket. He held it up. "Wanna see my magic blade?" He pushed a button causing a long, stiletto blade to slide into view.

"Whatta ya think of this, Fraser?" Chance waved the blade back and forth in front of Deke.

"Well, its O.K. if you like girl's knives." Deke said.

"Always the joker. Twice now you've had the upper hand on me, but three times is the charm." He thrust the knife into Deke's side and was standing uncertainly when Tommy, who had been talking to musicians on the bandstand, ran up, elbowed Callander in the mouth and dropped him to the floor.

Chance's hat went flying and he was crawling to recover it when an army boot came down on his hand. He screamed in pain causing the other Zoots to mill around like sheep. Without their leader, they were easy pickings for the soldiers, bouncers and crowd members who fell upon them. When the police arrived, the Zoots, in torn, bloodied clothing with swollen faces and bloody noses, clustered in a group on the dance floor apprehensively eyeballing their attackers. A collection of knives, cudgels, foreshortened pool cues and lead pipes were scattered on the floor.

Deke had energetically participated in the brawl -- Callander's knife had glanced off his metal cigarette case and inflicted a glancing wound that bled copiously but wasn't life-threatening. But, because he lost a fair amount of blood, he was hospitalized and didn't ship out with the regiment in December. Tommy, who had not completed his basic training, also stayed in Edmonton.

Deke was discharged from the hospital a week after the First Division had embarked for Britain. Placed on light duty, he spent his time keeping the barracks and offices in the Armoury clean. The only break was when the soldiers on base participated in hockey games. He and Tommy stood out amongst the players and their prowess did not do unnoticed by certain high-ranking officers.

Tommy received word that he was being transferred to Ontario at the behest of a colonel who was engaged in an inter-service hockey league. He would join a number of NHL players who were serving their country by playing hockey. Word had it that the league was very competitive and officers, in charge of the individual teams, were constantly scouting the ranks for good players.

Tommy chafed at being kept out of action to enhance some brass hat's hockey team and when Deke found out that he too had been scouted for a colonel's team, the friends began to search for a way of getting into action. They were considering desertion and reenlistment -- under assumed names -- when a mysterious soldier who introduced himself as 'Sergeant Messer' approached them.

Sergeant Messer was a Special Ops agent, who assured them that he could override their transfers. He was recruiting soldiers, who could think on their feet and handle themselves and, after an initial interview with the Sergeant, both boys volunteered for Messer's unit.

Soon, Tommy, Deke and a cadre of handpicked soldiers from other commands were subjected to extensive jump training, hand-to-hand combat instruction, marksmanship, and language training. They were told that they were to be dropped into countries that stood in the path of the Nazi juggernaut. Their mission was the extraction of 'boffins' -- British slang for scientists and academics -- from the threatened countries. Sometimes the boffins weren't that enthusiastic about relocation to Britain, Canada or other Commonwealth countries and extraordinary methods had to be employed. Some were Nazi sympathizers that had to be 'neutralized.'

Messer's unit operated as part of the S.O.E. (Special Operations Executive) and did most of its work in winter when frozen waterways could be used as escape routes. The unit's mandate also covered commando training for young Norwegians who would make up resistance elements after the invasion.

After the countries in question were invaded, and the so-called 'Phoney War' ended, the unit was downsized with members being returned to their original units. Tommy and Deke were transferred to the Eddie's base in England.

The following three years found the Eddies operating as a defense force in the British Isles. After Dunkirk, the Canadian army was the only fully manned and equipped force facing -- what was thought to be -- an imminent German invasion from continental Europe. However, the ensuing 'Battle of Britain,' was fought in the air and Canadian ground troops weren't committed to action until the Second Division participated in the ill-fated Dieppe Raid of 1942.

It wasn't until 1943 that the Eddies, as part of the Canadian First Division, saw action. The Division was delegated to be part of the British Eighth Army for Operation Husky, the invasion of Sicily and Italy. Highly trained and straining for action, the Canadians acquitted themselves admirably through Sicily and into Italy. The Italian Campaign was a brutal, mobile affair with the Allies pursuing the enemy from town to town, city to city.

On December 9, 1943 the Eddies, Seaforths and squadrons of Calgary Tanks together with companies of the 48th Highlanders of Canada established a bridgehead on the Moro River. The Edmonton regiment was detailed to proceed two miles north to a twelve-mile stretch of highway that linked the cities of Orsogna with the port city of Ortona. Upon reaching the highway they were to follow it to a crossroads within sight of Ortona.

Sergeant Tommy Flynn was a section leader in 'B' Company with Mitch Pawluk, Ihor Kovik, Lud Ludvigsen and five recent additions making up the section. Deke, also a sergeant, led a 'B' Company section that included, Peewee, Johnny Arvine, Hub Burke and five replacements. Dusty Midbo had been wounded during the Moro River crossing but to that time; none of the Calder boys had been lost.

As 2nd Brigade, including 'B' Company and the Calder boys, moved toward Ortona -- a city of stone on a promontory overlooking the harbour on the Adriatic Sea -- it was met with an obstacle that stopped them in their tracks. Called The Gully, it started as a narrow fissure in the earth and expanded to a steep sided ravine that measured 200 feet deep by 200 yards wide. Too narrow for tanks and artillery and, because the defenders were entrenched in the forward slope, difficult to combat with mortars.

The enemy, who had been dug-in in under the lip of The Gully, emerged and scythed down the first wave of advancing Canadians with machine gun fire. 'B' Company moved forward to the lip of The Gully but, with no way of crossing it, they dug in and waited for a solution.

While senior officers were pondering a way to cross The Gully, a combat team of the West Nova Scotia Regiment with Calgary tanks and British sappers encountered a laager of German tanks, which had been stationed to prevent a Canadian move to end-around the ravine. With the advantage of surprise, the combat team destroyed the German armour. At the same time, a company of Seaforths, operating with Ontario tanks, swung around The Gully in a wider arc and swept down the road toward Ortona until the tanks ran low on fuel and they withdrew to the Canadian lines with 100 German prisoners. The road to Ortona was open.

Domingo Romano was cowering in Rome's Cinecitta film studios during an Allied bombing, when an Italian Secret Policeman and a German SS man arrived. They said they were looking for actors who had a mid-Atlantic, North American accent or could simulate one. When asked why such actors were required, the policeman replied that the armed forces were filming a morale-boosting movie to be shown across Italy and Germany. As it dealt with war, the enemy had to be realistically portrayed.

Domingo had come a long way from his home in northern Alberta. He had followed his dreams and gone to Hollywood in 1924 as August Ouellette. Reinventing himself as Domingo Romano, he affected white suits and a Panama hat and when he made the rounds of casting offices, he always left a sheaf of 10"x12" glossies portraying him in pirate, desert sheikh and toreador costumes. In his mind he had done everything right. It would just be a matter of time before he was Rudolph Valentino's rival as a leading man. He had taken tango lessons and even learned to speak a smattering of Spanish.

After waiting in vain for work in major productions, he accepted a role in a Poverty Row film. He was cast as a Plains Indian chief, and subsequently began to get steady work in B movies. Hollywood studios never cast aboriginal Americans as aboriginal Americans. For some unexplained reason -- probably racism -- they favoured Mediterranean types over the real thing. Because of his Latin disguise, Domingo was able to make money in 'oaters.'

In 1939 several Italian filmmakers visited a film set where Domingo was portraying a Mexican vaquero in a supporting role. Something in his performance appealed to the Italians and they signed him to a contract. He was finally able to play the exotic roles he had gone to Hollywood to do. When the bombs started falling, Domingo, in the costume of a desert sheik, had been embracing a beautiful young woman in a set made up to look like a Bedouin tent. Thinking that a film, with such a wide distribution, could only help his career he volunteered and soon, with a group of male actors, he was driven to an area near Ortona. It soon became obvious that film work was not on the agenda when a German officer gave orders for the 'cast' to don British and Canadian uniforms, some blood stained, some with large rents in them.

German officers supervised the 'costuming' of the terrified actors in the malodorous uniforms. Each man was wired up with explosives and detonators and driven to an area where contact with advancing Canadian troops would be inevitable.

Domingo's mind raced. He knew that the Almighty was testing him and, somehow his talent for survival would see him through. He considered options such as dropping to the ground and losing himself in the rubble, or disabling the primitive explosive device strapped to his body and surrendering to his countrymen.

Inside of a partially demolished cathedral, German officers assembled their 'cast' of decoys and issued them with Canadian style helmets, non-functioning Tommy guns and Lee-Enfield rifles. They seemed to be short of boots, so Domingo and his companions wore their own footwear. The actors were to pose as victorious Canadians, bringing in German prisoners. The Germans 'prisoners' would be armed with concealed weapons and would approach the Canadians with arms aloft. When they were in close proximity to the Eddies, they would attack.

As Domingo was waiting for a divine message, a German officer pointed a luger at him and yelled raus, raus, indicating that he was to follow the ersatz prisoners into the debris field. The officer kept his arms behind his back and walked beside Domingo.

"Point your weapon at me you idiot," he hissed, and Domingo was complying when a red wound appeared between German's eyes and he flew backwards with an astonished look on his face.

Deke stood beside Helmer Lindquist, the unit's marksman. Helmer looked up and said: "Got the Kraut with his arms behind his back." Then, watching the procession wend its way toward them he added. "The other guys look like our boys with prisoners."

Deke played his binoculars on the approaching men. He watched the 'Canadians' for sometime, playing the glasses on their haircuts, clean hands and shiny shoes. He was about to commence firing when one of the 'Canadians' stumbled and his tunic opened, revealing explosives. Deke was lifting his Tommy gun when the man stopped, opened his tunic with both hands and called.

"Hey fellas. I'm Canadian. But these guys..." Domingo made a sweeping gesture to the men in Canadian uniforms, "are imposters. We're all booby-trapped." Without warning, he pulled the wires on his explosive device setting off an explosion that destroyed the top half of his body and took out two of the decoys and one of the German 'prisoners.'

A firefight ensued between Deke's detail and the German soldiers, who had dropped to the ground when Helmer shot their officer. After he and his section dispatched the enemy troops, Deke and his men continued on their mission to ferret enemy troops out of buildings in the city. As he looked down at the remains of Domingo Romano/August Ouellette, Deke said: "Nice shoes."

In the city -- which had been virtually destroyed by German demolition teams -- the Canadians found themselves up against the elite German First Parachute Division. Hitler had decreed that Ortona had to be held at all cost and a brutal slugging match ensued.

In preparation for the invading Canadians, the enemy blocked the main thoroughfares with debris to prevent tanks from moving into the city centre.

They also arranged rubble in such a way as to lead infantrymen into kill zones. With the streets under constant sniper fire, the Canadians countered with a Loyal Eddie invention called 'mouse holing.' The Canadians worked from house to house -- most houses in Ortona having common walls -- clearing one building and blasting a hole into the next with a satchel charge large enough to gain egress but small enough that it didn't bring the building down. They then would eliminate the forted-up enemy, floor by floor.

While Deke and his squad were mouseholing in one sector of the city, Tommy was assigned to lead a small unit of four men to a prearranged destination in another area of the city. He identified his objective and posted his men on the ruined balcony of a stone building. Then, he made his way to his primary objective.

Keeping a low profile, he ran with a stooped posture until he found cover behind a stone wall, where he fixed a piece of white cloth to a long wooden splinter of wood and held it above the wall.

"It's O.K. Canada I see your flag."

Tommy rose, ducked behind a higher wall segment, and moved around the corner where he came face to face with a large man in a knee-length airborne-issue camouflage jacket. The man, who had a Schmeisser machine pistol hanging at his chest, greeted him with a grin. "I once worked the Canadian National Railway in Jasper, Alberta."

"Oh yeah?" Tommy replied warily. "What

the hell's that got to do with the price of tea in China?"

"Ho, ho, ho." The German chortled. "I miss that smart-aleck Canadian sense of humour. "Come... come with me. You can keep your Tommy gun if you wish."

"You can count on that." Tommy said, "And, if you please, we'll just stay out in the open where my boys can see what's going on."

The paratrooper stepped over the ruins of a perimeter wall and pointed to what appeared to be a cellar door. He reached down and grasped a metal ring that rested in a circular recess and pulled the door up.

"Careful now," Tommy said cautiously and retreated several steps with both hands on his weapon. The paratrooper called down to someone in the cellar and soon the head of a child emerged. The German lifted the small figure to the surface and, over the next few minutes, seven small children were hoisted up out of the enclosure. A white-haired priest and a figure in a black nun's habit followed the children. The final figure to emerge was that of a young paratrooper who looked at Tommy and nodded.

The first paratrooper waved the young soldier out of the hole and returned the door to its closed position.

"Here they are as promised, Eddie. Our political officer has been diverted long enough for us to deliver them to you. He feels that they should be disposed of, but the Falschirmjager do not make war on children."

"Fallshim – what?"

"It is German for airborne." the man touched his field cap, which cast half of his face in shadow, and smiled. "Maybe we'll meet in the Rockies after the war?"

"Yeah, maybe," Tommy said absently as he turned to shepherd his flock back to the ruins that sheltered his squad. When he turned to look back, the Germans had disappeared.

Tommy caught up with the procession and took up a rearguard position. He noticed that the nun was shepherding the priest and the little ones toward Mitch who had come down to meet them. Tommy held his position until the children were in the building and then made for the entrance. He noticed that the nun stood in the doorway seemingly waiting for him to catch up.

"Geez," Tommy muttered audibly. "That is a husky nun."

"What's that my son?" The figure in the habit turned. "Something about my appearance that offends ye?"

Tommy looked up in surprise at the timbre of the nun's voice. As he approached, the figure in black reached out and grabbed him around the neck.

"I suppose you'll be wantin' to be confessing your many sins, you Calder lay about." The nun dragged Tommy through the doorway where the squad, weapons leveled at the struggling couple, confronted them.

Tommy reached out and removed the nun's cowl. The nun stood revealed as Billy Jurva.

"Stand down ya trigger happy goons." He grinned at them.

"Billy Jurva! I thought you were dead." Tommy said as the men gathered around. "What the hell are you doin' in the middle of this shit storm?"

Tommy watched as his old friend shucked the nun's habit to reveal himself in an American uniform.

"You better tell us just what the hell is goin' on here, Jurva. Why are you dressed like a Yank?"

"It's a long, long story. You know I went to Finland? Well, I got a little beat up and some friends of mine got me into Norway. From there I was put on a steamer from Stavanger Norway to Aberdeen Scotland. When I was back in shape I enlisted in the British Paras. When the Canadian Parachute Battalion was formed I transferred over to them. Now, I'm with an outfit called the First Special Service Force. We're a Canadian/American outfit. I like to say that we dress like Yanks but fight like Canucks.

I was detailed to go behind the Kraut lines to bring out Father Paduano -- who is an Allied agent -- and these Jewish kids, who were being sheltered in the church. Our Intel told us that the Gestapo was planning to raid the church to get the priest. We sure couldn't leave those little tykes there, so we brought everybody out.

"How'd you work out a deal with those Krauts?"

"Those two Kraut paras? They'll be showing up pretty soon. As soon as they give their uniforms back to the Krauts they tied up in the church."

Tommy's unit made their way, from building to building, skirting the rubble while shielding the priest and children and conducting them to a safe haven behind Canadian lines. At the site of a brewed-up tank, two soldiers in American uniforms joined them.

"Tommy looked closely at one of the newcomers. "Messer! I thought there was something familiar about you."

"Sergeant Messer grinned at him. "Pretty good imitation of a Kraut, eh? My family was German way back, so I can do the accent."

Tommy shook his head. "I should have known you'd turn up somewhere. You in the same outfit as Billy?"

"Yep. And this character, " he nodded at the other German impersonator, "is, Darcy Spotted Horse from the Blood tribe."

"That's Kainai to you. Paleface." The soldier grinned.

Sergeant Messer, Billy Jurva and Darcy Spottted Horse were members of a joint American/ Canadian commando unit, which had recently taken German positions that had previously been deemed impregnable. Because of their ferocity and a penchant for painting their faces black and infiltrating enemy lines at night, they had earned their famous nickname, "The Black Devil's Brigade."

After Tommy and the Special Service Forcemen were debriefed and the former hostages sent back down the line, Sergeant Messer caught up with Tommy and they discussed mutual comrades.

"Where's that crazy galoot, Fraser?" Messer asked.

"Oh, he's probably out blasting Krauts out of stone buildings somewhere."

"Well, we're going back to our unit tomorrow. Say hello to him for me."

"Will do."

The soldiers parted ways and Tommy was on his way to the mess hall when Captain Tymkow approached him. "Sergeant Fraser and his detail have been missing for hours. I want you to take out your boys at daybreak and see if you can find them."

"What about right now sir? My boys can be ready in minutes."

"Sorry Flynn," the captain said. "I can't risk losing any more men to what might be another Kraut setup. We've lost too many men to booby traps and mined buildings. In the daylight you can at least see what you're up against."

Soon after he left Captain Tymkow, Tommy saw a familiar figure approaching him. The man was covered in masonry dust and blood and was brushing his way past several stretcher-bearers who were attempting to restrain him.

"Tommy! Tommy! Wait up."

"Jesus, Peewee." Tommy reached out and caught the staggering man as he collapsed. "What happened? Where are Deke and the rest of your guys?"

Peewee sank to the ground at Tommy's feet. He reached out and gripped his friend's sleeve and looked imploringly at him before he lost consciousness. Tommy turned to the stretcher-bearers who were about to carry Peewee to the medical tent.

"Take care of him boys. I'll check in on him later."

Tommy made for the reserve area and searched until he came upon Billy's billet in a tent pitched inside a ruined office building.

"What's up Amici?" Billy said as Tommy entered. He was leafing through a book of English to Italian translation while reclining on a cot.

"How long you guys sticking around?" Tommy said.

"I'll ask the Commandante." He put down his magazine and shouted.

"Hey Mess."

The tent flap billowed and Messer emerged holding a shaving mug in one hand and a razor in the other. "What?"

"Tommy wants to know when we're leavin'."

"Hey Tommy," Messer nodded. "You got some nurses lined up or something?"

"Nothing that pleasant. Deke and his boys went out this morning. They were due back hours ago. Captain Tymkow is sending me out with my section at daybreak but Peewee Peterson just staggered in covered in dust and blood. He passed out before he could tell me where the boys are."

"Cut to the chase Paisano." Billy said.

"Well, I'm not waiting for daydreak. I'm going out in a few minutes.'

"Wait up," Billy said jumping to his feet. "Let me get my boots."

"I'd take my section -- I know they'd all volunteer -- but I don't want them to take the flak that will be coming down the pipe when the brass finds out I disobeyed orders."

"So, "Messer said, "You want us to go with you and get the shit on our shoulders?"

"Something like that. I've never seen anyone in this man's army that calls his own shots like you do."

"Well, my authority has its limits. What are you after?" Messer said.

"Billy is in your outfit. So, if you O.K. it Billy could come with me."

"What about me Flynn?" Messer said. "You're making me feel left out."

Tommy was silent for a moment, then he said: "You mean you're up for an unofficial patrol?"

"Well, this bozo," he nodded at Billy, "is one valuable, highly trained soldier. I just can't let him go gallivanting around without my supervision. Besides I owe you. You and Deke helped my ops successful back in '39. So, I'll tell you what I'll do. I'll go talk to Captain Tymkow and tell him that I'm borrowing you for a couple of hours as Darcy has already gone back to our unit. Meanwhile you go see if Peewee can give us any info."

Several hours later three dark figures slipped over the Canadian lines and made for a street in the hot zone. Peewee had been able to pinpoint the area before lapsing back into unconsciousness.

The trio moved quickly to the area designated by Peewee and found a street where three stone buildings had been reduced to rubble. They found Spitter Smatello on the street in front of the end house, more dead than alive. Spitter had been arrested for black-market activity in Edmonton and given an ultimatum. Sign up for active service or go to prison. He chose the former and surprised his contemporaries by becoming a competent infantryman. Chance Callander had opted for prison. The next man they found was Helmer Lindquist, half of his body crushed by a large stone slab. Inside, in the entryway, they came upon a soldier with no face. The body was missing the tip of a forefinger on its left hand and Tommy knew it to be Johnny Arvine. Zenon Kovik lay sprawled on the first landing -- a surprised look on his bluish white face. Billy stared at his childhood friend for several moments then made his way over a pile of rubble to toward his companions.

"Looks like Deke's boys were about to mouse hole these houses and the Krauts blew them up." Billy said.

"There's no sign of Deke." Messer said.

"Shh," Tommy said. "Hear that?"

"Yeah." Billy said. "A metallic sound. Something scraping. Like...hey! Look over there. A light."

Tommy peered into a narrow opening which emitted a faint light.

"Holy Christ!" Billy said. "There's someone down there."

They worked for an hour, digging with their hands and a salvaged coal shuttle. When they encountered a large stone lintel, blocking their way, the exhausted men realized that more help was required.

It took a platoon of sappers and a tank to finally remove the stone obstruction while infantrymen kept up a covering fire to keep the Germans pinned down. When the tank arrived to pull the lintel -- which had provided Deke with a protective shell -- out of the hole, Tommy and Bill dropped into the cavity and began removing smaller shards of stone and debris from around Deke.

"Geez am I glad to see you guys. I thought fer sure I was gonna be buried alive. When I heard sounds, I would light my lighter and scrape my cigarette case to make noise. I didn't even care if the was the Krauts that found me."

"Easy, easy." Messer said. "We have to dig out your foot so's you can dance again.

"Hey, Mess. Where'd you come from? Is that Billy? Jesus, what's going on? We all dead or something?"

"Hell no," said Tommy. You're alive and kicking. Anybody who can survive a stonehouse falling them has got to have a king-sized mojo working for him."

"Someone give me a hand with this rock," Sergeant Messer said attempting to free Deke's left foot. "We need something to lever it off."

Tommy applied a length of steel pipe to the stone that pinned Deke's foot.

"We've got you free except for your left foot." Billy said, "it might be busted up and you might be on crutches for a while. "

Deke's foot had been crushed. But the battle for Ortona was over. It was December 27th. The German paratroopers withdrew from the city that night thereby ending the battle that had been christened 'Little Stalingrad' by the press. Deke was invalided home, Tommy returned to his squad and Billy and Sergeant Messer returned to their unit. In the ensuing battles -- as the Eighth Army cleared the way to Rome only to stand down to allow the Americans to liberate it -- the Eddies fought in the forefront. Peewee Peterson recovered and was sent home but three more Calder boys; Mitch Mitchell, Bobby Bahniuk and Ranny MacDonald fell in ensuing battles.

Part 4

Chapter 12 – Casualties of War

DEKE, TOMMY, BILLY, IHOR, MITCH AND Peewee were gathered around their usual table in the Airport Hotel, when a man in the familiar striped cap and overalls of a railroader approached them. He stood behind Billy and addressed Deke.

"Hey Fraser, I just wanted you to know that I kicked your little slut out."

"What you yappin' about Perchuk?" Deke said.

"Edna...my ex." Perchuk sad. "Remember? You used to deliver gas bills back when you were still a kid. You always showed up when I was on shift, cuz ya always got a roll in the hay with the old lady. Well, I just wanted you to know that I tied a can to her cheatin' ass."

"Good for you Perchuk," Billy said. "Now why don't you take your dog and pony show somewhere else."

"Fuck you Jurva, I also came over to tell Fraser that he's sittin' next to the guy whose bin humping his stepmother fer years."

The remark hung in the air for several moments and Billy took the opportunity to stand up, spin Perchuk around and dog walk him to the door. He ran the protesting man through the entrance and pitched him onto the adjacent streetcar tracks. Perchuk landed hard and Billy waited until he saw the man sit up before he returned to the beer parlour. "Jeez," Deke said: " Why didn't he tell me something I didn't know?"

"You knew?" Tommy said. "All this time you knew. What about you Billy?"

"Pretty much about the time you showed up and you and Faith started dancing to all your records."

"And went to all those movies together." Deke added. He looked up to see Spitter Smatello standing behind Billy, twisting his railway cap in his hands.

"What's up Spitter?"

"Something you guys should know. Chance Callander is out of jail and raving about how Mrs. Fraser stole his whore from him. I think he's on his way to your house."

Faith had been standing at the sink when Rosie burst into the room and locked the door behind her.

"Chance is coming."

"Chance Callander? I thought he was in jail."

"Well I guess they let him out, 'cause he's coming

up the lane and he's yelling his head off." Rosie ran out of the kitchen and up the stairs.

Faith was drying her hands on her apron when she heard footsteps on the veranda. She opened a drawer, withdrew a butcher knife, and then called. "What do you want?"

"I want my Dara. I want my little whore. I know she's here."

"Dara hasn't lived here for years. She went overseas with the army."

Suddenly the door splintered and Callander came through the doorway.

"Yer lying. You bitch. You made a fool of my dad but you won't make a fool out of me."

"What do you mean?" Faith said as she concealed the knife behind her back.

"You bitch. You took my Dara away from me."

"She never was 'your Dara'," Faith said, "She hated you."

Chance launched himself at her and she didn't have time to react. He wrestled her to the floor and she was dismayed to hear the knife hit the floor.

"You took my Dara so now yer gonna be my whore. "

"You leave this house this instant. Get out!"

"I'm not leaving this house with my tail between my legs like my dad did. You ain't carrying' no rifle this time."

She was assailed by a gust of his alcoholic breath and a nauseous feeling formed in her stomach.

"Please... don't. You're drunk." Faith whispered. "The police are on the way."

"Just shut up." He said. Grabbing a handful of her hair he slammed her head against the floor until she blacked out.

Chance tore her apron off, grasped the neckline of her dress with both hands and tore it open. He was breathing raggedly as he pushed her brassiere up to reveal her breasts.

"I've always thought about screwin' you. Now," he panted. "I'm gonna."

He tore her dress until it was separated from neck to hem. Flipping back the torn sides of the garment, he was tugging at the waistband of her panties and undoing the buttons on his pants when he felt cold metal on his neck.

"Get off of her." Rosie said. "Get off of her or … I'll kill you."

Chance took his hands from Faith and raised them in the air. He turned slowly, swiveling his upper body, until his eyes met Rosie's. She held the old Ross with extended arms, its barrel staring him in the face.

"Hey Sis.' He smiled blearily at her. You've grown into quite a hot little number. When I'm through with her… I think I'll do you."

Deke saw Rosie's finger tighten on the trigger and he grasped the barrel and pushed it past his face as the weapon discharged.

Faith shuddered with the impact of the bullet as the recoil of the rifle spun it out of Rosie's hands. Rosie dropped to her knees at Faith's side and Chance -- sobered by the turn of events -- shakily gained his feet. Disoriented by the ringing in his

228

ears, he stared wide-eyed at the women for several moments then turned and gained his feet. He ran to the door to be confronted by Deke.

"Kill him Deke. Kill the dirty rotten bastard." Rosie screamed. "He killed Faith."

Deke grabbed Chance by his throat and saw the abject terror on his pallid, stubbled face.

Tommy rushed past Deke dropped to his knees beside Faith,

"How is she Rosie?"

"Oh Tommy. She's dead."

Billy ran into the parlour and returned with a blanket, which he gently placed over Faith's body leaving her face visible. He moved back and stood by Deke who threw Chance to the floor. Rosie approached Deke and Billy. "Are you guys going to kill Chance?"

"Sorry Rosie," he laid a hand on her shoulder. "Our killing days are over. The cops will get him and give him what he deserves. A hanging." Then he turned quickly, hiding the tears that ran down his face, and left the room. Billy stood with a boot on Chance's throat as Tommy telephoned the police.

Chapter 13 – Wild Bill

Resdelta N.W.T. Summer 1961

THE SKIPPER OF THE M.V. SLAVE eased his vessel over until it bumped gently against the rubber tires buffering the barge. Two deckhands leapt on to the barge's deck and secured lines fore and aft. Billy threw his gear onto the barge and helped the crew transfer supplies to the superstructure that served as the watchman's cabin.

When Bill and the cargo were safely on board the barge, the Skipper leaned out of a wheelhouse window. "Cast her off, boys." The deckhands unhooked the lines from the bollards, threw them on to the deck of the tugboat and jumped aboard while shouting farewells to their erstwhile passenger.

"Well, Billy Boy," the Skipper grinned down from the open window of the wheelhouse, as the tug began to move away. "If the black flies, or the no-see-ums, or the skeeters, or ...old Wild Bill, don't get ya ... we'll see ya next time. The Dew should be here tomorrow morning around oh six hundred, unless she gets weather-bound on the other side of the lake. Adios."

Bill experienced a pang of loneliness as he watched the towboat make its way across the delta toward a string of empty barges. He was en route to Norman Wells by river, to scout out possible well sites along the Mackenzie, and had to change to a boat that plied the big river. As he watched the Slave disappear into the evening gloom, he realized that he had enjoyed the company of the crew, now on their way upriver to Bell Rock, the company's shore station. During the two-day journey, Bill had joked, played cards and traded lies with members of the crew.

The M.V. Slave, a shallow-draught riverboat, pushed loaded barges downriver to the delta -- where the Slave River flowed into Great Slave Lake -- and moored them for pickup by the larger, more powerful vessels that supplied the settlements along the Mackenzie River. The riverboat's crew would lash the empty barges together and push the interconnected tow upriver to the company's shore station at Bell Rock.

During the trip downriver the crew had derived no end of glee, warning Bill of the eccentric watchman known as Wild Bill. They all had tales of the wild man who kept a solitary watch on the delta; the man who was to be Bill's host until the Radium Dew arrived in the morning. Rumor had it -- one deckhand told him -- that Wild Bill was actually Albert Johnson the notorious mad trapper of Rat River. Another theory had it that he was one of the MacLeod bothers who went missing in the Nahanni Valley years before.

He was regaled with stories of Wild Bill swinging through the trees in a loincloth a la Tarzan, battling bears with a sheath knife, and canoeing for miles up river before laying back and sunbathing as the current carried him back to the delta. One time he had apparently drowsed too long and found himself heading out into the storm-tossed lake. Wild Bill fought ten-foot swells and the lake's best efforts to swamp him, but brought his canoe back to the barge.

The upshot was; Wild Bill was strong as a bull, crazy as a shithouse rat, mean as a snake and somewhat sexually ambiguous. One toothless deckhand had cackled: "He's probably as horny as a three-peckered billy goat by now. So, if'n I was you, I'd keep my hands over my ass and my back against a wall."

Bill had laughed good-naturedly at the wild stories and colourful nose-stretchers, but now as he sat on his kitbag in the perpetual summer twilight of a northern summer, he began to feel uneasy. He lit a cigarette and -- when his eyes recovered from the flare of the match -- looked up to see a scarecrow-like figure standing in front of him.

"H-holy shit," Billy recoiled, inadvertently losing his cigarette and falling back between his bag and the wall of the cabin. While he struggled to his feet, using the cabin wall for support, he noticed that the man, whose head and face were covered by a shock of unruly white hair, had reached down and retrieved the cigarette.

"Ah," the man sighed. "A hard-centre. Ya' mind?" He held the cigarette up and looked quizzically at his visitor. Billy quickly fumbled a cigarette from a package that he fished from his shirt pocket. "Here, have a fresh one." The man happily exchanged the new smoke for the one that he held and waited patiently while Bill struck a match.

The flare of the match illuminated the man's face and Bill noticed a pair of lively brown eyes observing him as he held the match to the cigarette.

"Ahhh," the man exhaled a gust of smoke and smiled. "Nothing' like a tailor-made. I bin smoking roll-yer-owns far so long I'd forgotten what a good tight store-bought smoke tasted like.

"Here," Bill held out the package. "Keep it."

"Why thank you sir. You are a gentleman and a scholar." He held out a large hand to Bill and announced, "They call me 'Wild Bill'-- a moniker I don't mind too much -- and you must be the bird who is laying over for the Radium Dew?"

"Yes sir," Bill said. "I'm ..."

The man held up his hand palm out. "You don't have to tell me I know who you are."

"Oh yeah, I suppose Bell Rock must have radioed you about me."

"I don't need Bell Rock to tell me about someone I've known since he was a little kid."

Billy's head snapped back in surprise. "What?"

"I told you... I'm Wild Bill ... but, you ... you're Billy Jurva. Come inside ... I'll fire up the stove, and we can bullshit some." The man effortlessly picked up a heavy wooden crate of supplies and opened the cabin door. "Grab that other box of vittles, will yuh Billy? I'm so hungry I could eat the asshole out of a skunk."

Billy scooped up the second box of supplies and followed his host into the cabin. Wild Bill wore a frayed Cowichan sweater over a plaid shirt and corduroy trousers. The pants were tucked into a pair of rubber wellies. Billy's host moved to a cluttered table and began pumping air into a Coleman stove. He extracted a wooden match from a tin container on the wall and ignited the burners. Hefting a teakettle and finding it suitably heavy, he placed it on a burner. Glancing over his shoulder he grinned, "Pull up a chair Captain Jurva, take a load off. I'm just going to open up a can of stew ... you hungry?"

"No, not at all," Billy said quickly, "I had supper onboard the Slave."

"Well, more power to ya. This shit can't come up to old Bobby Ward's cookin.' I swear that man makes a Yorkshire pudding that will float right off your plate if you don't spear it with a fork." Wild Bill twisted the handle of a can opener and opened a can, which he then dumped into the saucepan on the burner. Billy sat watchfully puffing on a cigarette while his brain laboured to place the man.

"Instant coffee O.K.?" Wild Bill asked waving two tin mugs. Billy nodded absently and the man spooned several teaspoons of the ersatz substance into each of them. Wild Bill snickered and added, "Still can't figure out who I am, eh?"

"Christ, you can't be ... Ewan?"

The man grinned set down the cups and made an exaggerated bow. "In the flesh young Billy ... in the flesh."

"Jee-zus," Billy kneaded his brow. "We all thought you were dead ... all these years."

"Sorry to disappoint. But I have been alive. All these years."

"No, no." Billy protested. "I didn't mean it that way. I'm not disappointed."

"Ah, I know you aren't." Ewan's voice softened as he poured hot water into both cups. He returned the kettle to the stove and pulled up a chair and sat down across the table.

"Jesus, when was the last time I saw you?" Billy asked. '38. '39?"

"Somewhere before the war. Sometime before you went to Finland. I went to Blighty in '39. Got smashed up in a wreck when the Jerries bombed a marshalling yard in Scotland."

"Faith thought you were dead. We all thought you were dead."

"Oh, that's right. You were Faith's great admirer weren't you? Good for you. She was worth your affection."

"If she was worth my affection," Billy asked hotly, "why wasn't she worth your affection?"

"You don't know do you? All these years and you don't know."

"Don't know what? That you had the kindest, most beautiful women in the world as your wife and you deserted her?"

"God, Billy, how often I wished that I could have felt the way you did about her. I did love her. But I couldn't manifest my love for her. After we were married, she expected that I would tend to her and maybe give her some kids but it just didn't work. I finally broke down and told her that I had sustained a 'Jake Barnes' injury during the war..."

"Jake Barnes. The character from 'The Sun Also Rises?"

"Yeah, you know. The guy who was rendered impotent by a war wound."

"Did that happen to you?"

"No. But that was my cowardly way of dealing with it. We actually did sleep together but the best I could do was to hold her and keep her warm. I often thought, as I lay there as she slept in my arms, that I was envied by the red blooded Calder boys who would have given anything to be lying next to that beautiful woman." Ewan stood and returned to the stove. He picked up the saucepan and stirred its contents for several seconds before dumping it into a bowl. He dug a spoon out of a drawer and, bringing his meal to the table, sat down and smiled at Billy.

"Have another smoke, drink your coffee and

relax while I eat. Then, I'll tell you anything you want to know."

Billy sipped his coffee and watched Ewan ladle the canned stew into his mouth. He appeared to enjoy his questionable fare and after he had cleaned the bowl with a piece of bread he pulled a cigarette from the pack on the table and began searching his pockets. He produced a familiar looking bullet-shaped lighter, took off the cap and thumbed the wheel. The wheel produced a spark but the wick refused to light. Bill struck a match and reached over the table and lit Ewan's smoke.

"Shit, I should have ordered some lighter fluid."

Ewan leaned back and exhaled a plume of smoke toward the ceiling before sitting up and placing his elbows on the table.

"I'll give you a short history of the fabled Fraser clan. I was two years older than my brother Callum but he outgrew me when we were in our teens. My dad, Malcolm, was a boxing fanatic. The greatest day of his life was when he went down to Calgary to watch Arthur Pelkey and Luther McCarty fight for the white heavyweight championship of the world. Jack Johnson was the real heavyweight champ but no white man was about to beat him.

Any way, Pelkey dropped McCarty in the first round and the old man was at ringside when everybody realized that McCarty was never going to get up again ... being as how he was dead. The old man dined out on that story for the rest of his life.

In the early years -- when I was a little kid -- it seems to me that we were happy on the old homestead. My mother was a dour, competent woman who allowed me to spend a lot of time with her. In fact I spent more time in the kitchen with my mother than my dad thought was seemly. As I grew older -- and didn't show any signs of changing -- Malcolm started to get nervous. Hugs and signs of physical affection were terminated by both of my parents and Callum was given free rein to toughen me up."

"Toughen you up. How?"

"Well... Malcolm would get Callum to goad me and push me around until I struck back in self-defense. At that point Malcolm would declare that we settle it in the ring. We'd put on the gloves and Callum would proceed to kick the living shit out of me. I wasn't much of a challenge for him because I would never lift my gloves to protect myself. I can still hear him screaming at me, 'Fight you sissy. Hit back. C'mon you big pansy, stand up for yourself."

"What about your mother? Didn't she stand up for you?"

"My dear mother?" Ewan chuckled ruefully. "I discovered later that she had also been uncomfortable with my behaviour. When I came to her with black eyes and bruises, the best she would offer me was, 'Och laddie, ye've got tae be strong tae survive. Ye cannae be a sissyboy. Callum will keep after ye' until ye' fight back. So, pool yersel' taegether and act lak' a mon.'"

"Did you ever retaliate?"

"One day, when the family and some neighbours gathered for a card that featured some neighborhood boys that Malcolm coached. The main event was to be Callum and me. Tired of the regular shit kicking, I decided to put an end to my misery. I went into the tool shed, found a section of bicycle chain and wrapped it around my right fist. I pulled my gloves on and waited for a bout to finish before climbing into the ring to face Callum.

The audience was on the veranda sipping beer and lemonade as they watched Callum and I circle each other. Malcolm was the referee and he had just given us our instructions and had us touch gloves. We came together in the centre of the ring and my brother walked confidently over to me with his hands hanging at his sides. 'Come and get it Ewan-da,' he said. Malcolm told him to shut up and get at it and, as Callum made a big show of winding up to hit me, I moved up and clocked him between the eyes with my chain-enhanced fist.

Well sir, he went down like a ton of bricks with this shocked look on his face. He was out for something like twenty minutes. Malcolm had to restrain me from hitting him when he was down and when he grabbed my right hand to lift it in the air; he felt something under the glove.

"What did he say about the chain?"

"Not a thing. He just muttered something like 'Anything that works. Anything that works.'"

"So he condoned your dirty fighting?"

"Yep, I think he was gratified that I had a mean streak. At least it was a manly way to do things, he thought. He was happy to see that his sissy boy son had exhibited some 'good' qualities. It was a breakthrough in his eyes."

"So you changed?"

"Yep, I became what dear old dad wanted me to be, a two-fisted brawler. After awhile people started giving me a wide berth -- if they thought I was even mildly pissed off -- because they knew I was a loose cannon who fought dirty and would do anything to win."

"But, didn't it go against your nature?"

"I changed my nature. I submerged it in the so-called manly pursuits. I played hockey and learned to love the sport. I played football, lacrosse and became a better than average boxer. Believe me, I made my family forget that I ever liked to play with dolls. The only problem was, deep inside? I still wanted to play with dolls."

"So," Billy said. "Through sheer willpower you overcame your cravings?"

"Nah, I never really overcame them -- they were always with me. Although there was a time, just before the first war, when I had a girlfriend and was even contemplating marriage. I had this temporary conceit that I could will myself to be 'normal.' Anyway the war showed up and got me off the hook."

"So, you viewed the war as an escape?"

"Yes I did. Like a lot of poor fools I signed up early to avoid the rush. As terrible as the fucking war was -- and it was indescribably terrible -- it provided me with a wonderful part of my life."

"How could anything good come out of that god forsaken war?"

"Well, number one: I got out from the restraints of my family and the social strait jacket I was in. Number two: I was able to meet my one true love. Now don't get nervous Billy -- I know it embarrasses you -- but it is something that has to be said."

"Believe me Ewan there is not a hell of a lot in this world that embarrasses or surprises me anymore. I've been through the meat grinder twice and I've seen more than my share of human frailty."

"Thank you Billy, I'm relieved. Anyway, when my unit arrived at Valcartier, I discovered that the army was desperately looking for diversions to keep the troops occupied. So many volunteers flooded the place, in such a short time that the brass couldn't cope. Sports, especially boxing, became a big thing and my ring experience earned me a spot on the battalion boxing team. While the rest of the sweats were on long route marches or engaging in hours of square bashing and bayonet drills, I was in the gym."

"Sounds like a pretty good berth."

"Oh, I was forced to do some basic training, but on the whole I had it pretty good. Knowing what my buddies were going through I mentally thanked the old man for teaching me how to fight. I won a brigade boxing championship before I shipped out and some Colonel Blimp in Blighty felt that I would look good in his boxing program so I was transferred to his outfit.

When I got to the battalion in England, I found a young officer waiting for me. He introduced himself as Roland Campion. He told me that he was in charge of pugilism for the Canadian Expeditionary Force. This fellow told me that I was now in a sports battalion where I would train for an inter-service championship match."

"What was your weight class?"

"I was a heavyweight."

"How did you do?"

"Not bad, not bad at all. I more than held my own at the inter-service championship level. One time I went to the finals and lost on a split decision. The next time I came up against a real tough guy who kayoed me in the third round. But I became well known in military and betting circles and began to travel in some pretty fast company. Through Roland, I met and attended parties with everyone from dukes and duchesses to music hall girls and bookies. Roland was the second son of a hereditary baronet up on the Scottish border and he had impressive contacts in London society.

After serving in a regiment of lancers during the South African War, Roland had spent a few profligate years spending his father's money until his dad, Sir Alban, exiled him to Canada. He spent some time working on ranches and playing polo but when the war started he signed up with the Pats and was back in the old country in the fall of 1914. He could have gone back to Blighty, rejoined his old regiment and regained his rank but preferred serving with Canadian troops. He always called Canadian troops the 'Flowers of the Forest' because of the quality of men that came from such a wild country.

The Pats went into action in France in early 1915 and Roland lost a leg at Frezenberg. He spent six months in hospital and was given a wooden leg and the job of organizing sporting events for the C.E.F."

"This guy, Roland. Was he your great love?"

"Within minutes of meeting we knew that we had the same disposition and, for the first time in my life, I realized that there were others out there just like me. People like Roland who accepted their fate and learned to live with it. Hell, maybe even dared to enjoy it. I won't embarrass you with the details Billy, but Roland was not only my lover, he was also my mentor. He taught me everything from how to use a knife and fork to an appreciation of good food, good wine, good music, and even poetry for Christ sake! Roland's favourite poet was Arthur Rimbaud and he took great pains to educate me in French poetry because it was our intention to settle in Paris after the war. You can see," Ewan waved to a corner of room where crowded bookshelves were affixed to the wall above his bed. "The lessons stuck"

"What happened between you guys?"

"Well, Roland's older brother Edmond was killed at the Somme in 1916. Soon after that, Sir Alban, died of a massive stroke. Roland maintained it was caused by a fit of apoplexy at the thought of his queer son being heir to the title. Anyway, Roland left for the north to attend his father's funeral and assured me that he had every intention of returning to London within the week but I never saw him again."

"What happened?"

"Roland had told me that he was looking forward to telling his mother, Lady Edwina, that he was going to relinquish the title. He knew that she was going to hit the ceiling, because with him out of the way, the estate, title -- and everything that went with it -- would shift to his cousin who would install his own family in the mansion. Roland's mother wouldn't have been thrown out on the street but she would have had to exist in reduced circumstances."

"Jesus," Billy said. "Couldn't he have helped his old mum out by hanging on to the title?"

"I guess he could have, but Roland and his mother never had what you would call a warm relationship. Both he and his brother had been brought up by a succession of nannies, governesses and tutors while their parents hung around with the likes of the Prince of Wales. Any maternal feelings Edwina had were directed to his brother Edmond. Roland put that down to sheer self-service as Edmond would succeed his father one day and she would need his good will. Roland told me she barely tolerated him during his childhood and when she learned of his lifestyle preferences she treated him like a pariah in spite of the fact that a number of people in her own circle were openly homosexual."

"So it was payback time?"

"Oh yes. Roland made no bones about it. He was looking to get back at her. Edwina apparently had an inkling of his intentions though, because she had some of the local lads lock him up in the castle."

"She kidnapped him?"

"Yeah, she held him for ransom. She decided to hold him until she could convince him to take the title and make things right. The only problem was... Roland knew the castle like the back of his hand. Within minutes of being locked up, he was out on the sill of his third floor window. As boys, Edmond and Roland had scaled the stone walls of the house and knew every nook and cranny on the face of the old structure. The only trouble was, in order to make his way down the wall, Roland needed two hands and two working legs."

"He fell?"

"Yes ... he fell."

"How did you find out about it?"

"Roland had a valet, Vincent Eames, who, like many members of his family, had worked for the household. When Roland arrived from Canada with the Pats he arranged to have Vincent taken on strength as his batman. Vincent wasn't one of us but he was fanatically loyal to Roland, as they had played together as small boys. When Roland was imprisoned, Vincent went to the local constabulary and told them of trouble at the mansion. By the time he and a constable arrived, Roland had already fallen to his death."

"Jesus! How did Lady Macbeth take it?"

"She died soon afterward. Drowned in the loch I hear. Vincent told me that it was ruled an accident but considered a suicide."

"So where did that leave you?"

"Well. I could have stayed where I was and spent the rest of the war in the boxing ring. But, the loss of Roland took the starch out of me. I decided that I didn't want to live anymore and volunteered for active service in France. My strategy was to let old Fritzie kill me. That way I wouldn't have to commit some messy form of suicide. Within days, I was in the meat grinder, as you so aptly call it, and kicking myself for not putting a pistol in my mouth back in Blighty."

"Mingo told me about trench warfare."

"Believe me Billy. No one can really explain it. It was a totally indescribable experience. It truly was hell on earth. You've seen your share of action, but have you ever watched rats tear away at the bodies of your friends? Have you ever stood for days in a knee-deep mixture of mud, shit, blood and decomposing bodies? Have you seen men cut down in the hundreds and left to rot into the ground?"

"No, no I haven't. Mingo said much the same thing."

"Mingo went through a hell of a lot more than I did. He was incensed by the cold-blooded ignorance of the high command. You'd shake your head and say to yourself, 'surely they're not going to send us into that wire, or that machine gun fire, or that mud ... but they always did. We came to care more for poor old Fritzie, in the lines facing us, than we did those cowardly red-tabbed bastards that sent us out to die, day after bloody day."

"Mingo told me he saw the foot soldiers, on both sides, as pit bulls who had a lot in common but were forced to fight each other to the death."

"An apt analogy."

"So what happened to your plan to get yourself killed?"

"As you can see, it obviously didn't work. All it did was get me mentioned in dispatches. You see, in the front lines a suicidal soldier is not such a bad thing. My efforts, in trying to get killed, made me appear to be a brave, hell-for-leather hero. I volunteered for trench raids, scouting parties, and sniper duty. I always was a good marksman and my performance on the range was recognized and got me assigned to a sniper detail. I was sent over to the Pats where I worked with two legendary snipers, Francis Pegahmagabow and Jim Christie. Both of them were hunters in real life and they taught me the fundamentals of the trade."

"So you served with Mingo?"

"No, I didn't meet Mingo until after the war. Callum was in the cavalry -- in the same unit as Mingo -- and, just before a cavalry charge he gave your uncle a package to hold for safekeeping. It was a package of French postcards for Malcolm. Anyway, Callum and most of his fellow cavalrymen didn't survive that charge so, sometime after the war Mingo showed up at the house with the package. He brought Faith with him.

"I remember hearing about that. So, when were you wounded?"

"Easter of 1917. Vimy Ridge. I caught a load of shrapnel in both legs. From April of '17 to March of '18, I was in a French hospital having pieces of metal picked out of my legs and having one rebuilt. After that, I spent another six months convalescing in London and, when I could stagger around without the use of a cane, the army decided to transfer me to a railway battalion because of my civilian experience. My mail caught up to me before I debarked and I learned that Callum had been killed. When I got home the old man was waiting for me at the depot and he started campaigning for me to rebuild the family."

"What happened to your mother?"

"She died of the Spanish flu in 1919. One week before I got home."

"What did you say to your dad about raising a family?"

"I must admit that I took the easy way out. I told him-- the same thing that I told Faith some years later – that I had been rendered impotent by shrapnel."

"How did he take it?"

"Not well. Not well at all."

"Mingo didn't tell me much about that period of time. Do you know why he brought Faith to Edmonton?"

"Faith's people were Mormons from around Milk River. Apparently these Jack Mormons, as Mingo called them, were all for the good old days when a man could have as many wives as he wanted. Faith had been selected to be the wife of some old fart and she got word to her brother Abel and he engineered a rescue with the help of Mingo and the Mounties. Abel arranged to have her live with a family in Calgary before he enlisted.

Some kerfuffle on the commune caused a number of members to break away and set up across the line in Montana. Apparently the leader of the breakaways -- who called himself a Prophet -- had decided that Faith's betrothal was an act of God, and must be realized. The only trouble was... he couldn't find her.

After the war, Mingo and Abel were looking for a way to make some money and began smuggling Canadian booze to thirsty Yanks during the Prohibition Era. They bought themselves some mules and began making good money but on their last trip some Yanks, pretending to be lawmen, ambushed them. These phoney deputies were to delay the boys until the Prophet -- who grabbed Faith when she went to Milk River to visit her mother -- had a chance to get over the border. Abel and Mingo overcame the deputies and, taking a shortcut intercepted the Prophet and his crew. Mingo didn't go into great detail about what happened next... only that he brought Faith back."

"So you married her soon after?"

"Well, yes. I did marry Faith. But there were mitigating circumstances. Mingo told us that these cultists believed that God's Law, as handed down by their Prophet, could not be rescinded. That meant that they wouldn't stop coming after Faith as long as she was single. The only way out for her was a marriage recognized by the government."

"That must have made your dad happy."

"Happy? He was overjoyed."

"Was Faith happy about it?"

"I think the word would be thankful."

"Deke must have been around at that time."

"He was six or seven at the time. Malcolm was happy with Deke, after making a fuss when the little guy was dropped on our doorstep, he thought the world of the boy. Being Callum's child, he looked just like us.

"One thing that has always puzzled me is the way Faith treated Deke." Billy said.

"Well, as I told you. We Frasers all look alike. I look like Malcolm. Callum looked like me and Deke looks like all of us. Anyway, I haven't told you about my father's predilection for young women have I?"

"No, you haven't."

"When Deke was a little shaver, we had a succession of nannies and housekeepers around the place. Most of them didn't last long because Malcolm was always trying to corner them and get them into bed. Some of them went along with it. Most didn't. They would just quit. When Faith showed up, in need of a husband, Malcolm thought he had a hold on her. He knew that she had no place to go and couldn't afford to be seen as a single woman so he made the poor girl's life miserable. I was of no help at all. Finally, she threatened to tell Mingo of Malcolm's machinations and that seemed to alleviate matters. He left her alone after that. I am afraid that Faith found all Fraser men wanting. Malcolm was a satyr, I was indifferent and Deke had the misfortune of looking like both of us."

"Poor Deke, Billy said. "I remember him trying his damndest to get a smile out of her. That was the only thing about her that saddened me. Her treatment of my best friend."

"Yeah, you poor little buggers," Ewan sighed. "I always thought of you guys as prairie thistle."

"Prairie thistle?"

"Yeah, you know, that tough wiry little plant that grows in the harsh environments on very little sustenance.

There you were, an orphan from the bald-headed prairie, and Deke, an orphan with two defacto parents. After your parents and then your aunt died, you never thought you were worthy of anyone's love. When Faith smiled upon you, you elevated her to the status of a saint. Deke went from woman to woman but never found what he was looking for. In spite of all that I've decided that you guys weren't thistles at all ... you were also Flowers of the Forest."

"What about Tommy? "

"Ah, he was a bloody hothouse flower. He was pouting over the treatment he got from the Leafs so he ran away and enlisted. Then there was the other business ..."

"Yeah, let's not talk about that."

"I agree. Let's not."

They talked until the M.V. Radium Dew bumped up against Ewan's house barge in the morning. As his gear was being loaded onto the deck of the Dew, Billy looked around for Ewan.

"You lookin' for Wild Bill?" a deckhand asked.

"Yeah, I wanted to say goodbye to him."

"Well, yer too late. As we were pulling up I saw him untie his canoe and get in it."

"Which way did he go?"

"He was paddling upriver."

Epilogue

DEKE BECAME AWARE OF A FIGURE emerging from the cloud of smoke and ice fog, as he busied himself under the hood of his old Ford coupe. During his midnight to eight a.m. shift, he had come out several times to start the car and let the engine warm up. He wanted to make certain that it would fire up at quitting time and take him home where his belongings stood ready to be stored until he returned from Japan. His old friend and army buddy Sergeant -- now Captain -- Messer, had offered him a posting in Tokyo where he would help prepare U.N. soldiers for service in Korea. He was ready for a change. There was nothing to keep him in Edmonton any longer. Rosie and Billy had moved to Calgary and Ihor and his wife, and growing family, were living in the old Fraser house, which Deke had leased to them at a reasonable rate. His old crowd had been diminished by the war; Tommy had disappeared after Faith's death. Ihor said that someone had told him that he had been seen with a touring hockey team in Ontario. Billy was doing well in the oil business. Most of the surviving Calder boys had settled into domesticity. Mitch Pawluk had taken university courses on a DVA grant, became a civil engineer and was married to Dulci Flynn. Most of vets went back to the railway but Deke felt a restlessness that could only be assuaged by getting away and, to that end; he enlisted in the Princess Pats for duty in Korea.

He was adjusting the throttle linkage on the carburetor when he sensed someone at his elbow. The man was speaking but the sound of the revving motor drowned out his voice. Deke allowed the motor to drop back to an idle then looked up.

"Hey there pardner." the man said in a raspy voice. "Can you spare some coin and maybe a smoke for an old vet?"

Deke had heard that line a hundred times since the war. Hobos --passing themselves off as veterans to win some sympathy from the rail workers -- were constantly panhandling in the yard. He was normally sympathetic but lately, he had begun asking the so-called veterans where they had served.

"Italy, mostly," was the man's answer. "Liri valley, the Sangro, the Moro River. Adriatic coast."

"Whereabouts on the Adriatic?"

"Ortona."

Deke stood up, slammed the hood down, and turned to the man.

"You were in Ortona?"

The man nodded and Billy thought he detected

a flicker of recognition in his eyes. He moved up and peered closely at the ragged man.

"Jesus! Tommy! Is that you?"

The man dropped his eyes and shook his head slowly back and forth. "No, no," his voice had a harsh rasping quality, "all I need is six bits and maybe a smoke if you can spare one." He seemed eager to escape Deke's scrutiny.

Reaching under his heavy coat Deke dug some bills out of his inside pants pocket and held them out. The man shuffled towards him and shyly selected several singles from his hand.

"Take it all," Deke protested. "It's yours."

"No, this is all I need. Honest."

"Well at least take some smokes," Deke held out a crumpled pack of Buckinghams. Deke watched as the man stowed the money and cigarettes into pockets of his tattered army greatcoat.

"Jesus man, you'll freeze to death in this weather. Take some more money ... get yourself a room."

"No," I'm fine. Thanks a lot. I won't forget this ... Deke."

"Goddammit! It is you." Deke whooped and grabbed the man's arm. "You had me goin' for awhile. Tommy, for Christ's sake! What the hell you up to? I haven't seen you in a dog's age."

"I'm not up to anything Deke." Tommy looked down at his ragged clothes and then raised his eyes. "This is me! This is what I am."

"Bullshit! You're no fuckin' rubbie ... you're the Fireball for Chrissake. No, you're coming with me.

We'll get something to eat at the cafe, then we'll go to my place and get you cleaned up and into some decent kit. I got a million questions to ask you. Get in the car and wait for me. I'm off in half-an-hour."

"Deke, please let me go." Tommy pleaded as he pulled away from his friend's grip. "I can't go with you. The cafe wouldn't let me in the door."

"Then, we'll get you cleaned up first."

"O.K. Deke. Tell you what. I've got my kit over in the roundhouse. I'll go get it. You pull around when you're off shift and I'll meet you out front … O.K.?"

"Good," Deke shook his head vigorously. "Tell you what! You go get your kit, then come back to the car and fire it up. Key's are in the ignition. There's brass monkey balls on the ground this morning so just relax and get warm."

Tommy nodded his assent and made his way toward the roundhouse as Deke headed toward the yard office.

When his shift was completed, Deke returned to his car to find the Ford idling smoothly, emitting a plume of exhaust smoke into the cold morning air. The car was empty.

Deke drove out of the yard and turned west. He drove one block to the roundhouse and sat waiting for his friend. When Tommy didn't show up after a half hour, he left the car and made his way into the large brick building. Consulting with many acquaintances he searched the building. No one remembered seeing Tommy.

As he began making his way back to the entrance he heard someone call his name and waited as one of the machinists approached him.

"Deke, they tell me you're looking for Tommy Flynn. Tell me that the rubbie I've been letting sleep in a tool crib isn't him."

Deke described Tommy and the man shook his head sadly.

"I can't fuckin' believe it! That sorry son of a bitch is the Fireball."

"Tell me," Deke grabbed the man's arm. "Where is this tool crib?"

The man led the way to a small room adjacent to a large mountain locomotive, which was undergoing a major overhaul. The machinist pointed to an area under a chest-high workbench, which ran across the short wall of the room.

"I've bin lettin' the pore bugger kip here while the weather is so fuckin' bad. I can't believe he's Tommy Flynn."

Deke leaned over and surveyed a tangle of ragged blankets, burlap sacks and cotton waste. Something caught his eye and he reached down and retrieved a flat object attached to a cardboard bad order tag. He read the scrawled words. 'This is for you Deke ... you should have it. I know you'll come looking ... but I don't want to be found. Ciao Amici, Tommy.'

"Jesus H. Christ! Deke examined the item and fell back against one of the locomotive's giant wheels. In his hand was a tattered photograph of Faith."

Calder Nuisance Ground
December 25th 1951

An overnight dump of snow had transformed the irregularly shaped mounds of garbage into a series of softly contoured hills. The snowfall had also invested the area with a cloying odour after extinguishing a number of fires scattered throughout the nuisance ground.

A figure in an ankle length buffalo coat stood on one of the mounds and, when he saw two vehicles enter the grounds, waved his arms to attract the attention of the drivers. He watched as the vehicles changed direction and began to rock their way over the frozen terrain towards him.

A black unmarked Ford sedan preceded a panel van -- bearing Edmonton Police Department markings -- to the designated area. Two plainclothes officers in the lead vehicle surveyed the landscape through celluloid frost shields on the interior of the windshield.

"Jesus, what a stink! It gets into yer nostrils and stays there all day." Fred Stevenson said from behind the wheel of the Ford. He wrinkled his nose in distaste and turned to his companion, "Gotta a smoke?"

Raymond Poole removed a glove and fished a pouch pack of Buckinghams from a pocket of his fur-collared Station Wagon coat. He shook the pack until the end of an unfiltered cigarette emerged. He extended it to Fred who reached over and lipped it out of the pack. Fred held his position until Raymond pocketed the smokes and held out a Ronson lighter to light the cigarette.

"Ain't you lightin' up?" Fred asked, exhaling a gust of smoke.

"Nah," Raymond said. "I've smelled worse."

"Yah, I suppose you have. Where'd you serve?"

"Italy. Finished up in Holland."

"I hear them Dutch girls are pretty good looking.'

"You mean the ones that weren't starving to death?"

"There's Hitch," Freddie said, happy to change the subject. He pointed a mitted hand at Constable Jack Hitchcock, the officer responsible for the Calder district. Hitch indicated where he wanted them to park and Freddie steered the car to the base of the mound, placed the gear lever in neutral, and left the motor idling as he and Raymond began adjusting their clothing for the -30 temperatures that awaited them.

The panel truck pulled up behind the Ford and two officers in winter-issue greatcoats and fur-lined, helmet-style caps, emerged, expelling gusts of vapour as they opened the back door of the van and removed a canvas stretcher.

"So...where's the stiff?" one of the uniforms asked.

"I would assume that it's somewhere up there with Hitch," Freddie pointed up at the hill above them where Hitchcock was shaking out a coil of knotted rope.

"Tie that stretcher to the end of this," Hitch said, "I've got the other end secured up here."

He swung the coil over his head several times and released it. The men watched it arc into the air and land at Raymond's feet. He nodded to the uniforms, who looped the rope through one of the iron legs of the stretcher.

When the stretcher and all of the policemen were on the mound, Hitchcock conducted them to an area where several burlap bags partially covered a figure, whose sheepskin-lined flight boots, protruded from the bags.

"I covered the poor bugger." Hitchcock said as he removed the bags covering the corpse. "Two kids with brand new Red Ryder BB guns were plinking in the dump when they found him."

Raymond Poole knelt beside the body. "I know this guy. Served with him in Italy. Y'know, he once played for the Leafs. You have probably heard of him. Fireball Flynn."

Addendum

―――――――――――――――――――――――――――――――――

CHANCE WAS ECSTATIC. HE LIFTED THE scented note to his nose inhaled and smiled radiantly.

"My Dara is back," he said aloud. "My little whore is coming back. I *knew* she would."

He had checked his mailbox this morning and had cried with pleasure at the name on the note. She was coming to him. His old dad had once told him that women like rough treatment and he was right.

Chance had returned to Edmonton, after doing a long stretch in the Stoney Mountain Pen in Manitoba, for manslaughter in the death of Faith Fraser.

He had spent the morning cleaning up the place. He had even taken a bath and scared up some clean clothes. He whistled and sang his way through the day until he heard a car pull into the yard. His heart was in his mouth as he met her at the door.

As he turned to conduct her into his house,

Dara slid a scalpel from her handbag and moved up behind him.

"She's coming out." Rosie Jurva said to Dulci Flynn-Pawluk, who sat behind the steering wheel. She drove the car to the front door of the house and waited for Dara to emerge.

Dara ran to the car, opened a back passenger door, and sagged back against the seat.

"It's done." She said.